祕密間諜

The Secret Agent

原著 _ Joseph Conrad　　改寫 _ Donatella Velluti　　譯者 _ 劉嘉珮

ABOUT THIS BOOK

For the Student

🎧 Listen to the story and do some activities on your Audio CD.

💬 Talk about the story.

⭐ Prepare for Cambridge English: Preliminary (PET) for schools.

(FACT FILE) Read informative fact files which develop themes from the story.

(LIFE SKILL) Draw comparisons between the story and contemporary life.

 Go to Helbling e-zone to do activities.

For the Teacher

HELBLING e-ZONE — A state-of-the-art interactive learning environment with 1000s of free online self-correcting activities for your chosen readers.

Go to our Readers Resource site for information on using readers and downloadable Resource Sheets, photocopiable Worksheets, and Tapescripts.
www.helblingreaders.com

For lots of great ideas on using Graded Readers consult Reading Matters, the Teacher's Guide to using Helbling Readers.

CONTENTS

Joseph Conrad was born in 1857 in Berdychiv (Ukraine). At the time the city was part of the Russian Empire, but before that it was part of Poland. He came from a Polish family of intellectuals[1] and political activists who fought for the reunification[2] and independence of Poland. So he was Russian, but he considered himself Polish.

He wasn't a good student at school, but he read a lot of novels, poems and Shakespeare, and he spoke French perfectly. He showed a great talent as a storyteller[3] from a very early age. At 16 he joined the French merchant navy[3] first, and later the British one. Over 19 years he worked on many ships, traveled the world and reached the rank of captain.

He suffered from[4] bad health and from clinical depression[5] all his life. At 20 he even tried to kill himself. In 1886 he became a British citizen. In 1894 he left the merchant navy and became a writer. Two years later he married an English woman, Jessie George, and they had two sons.

Although English was Conrad's third language and he only learnt it from the age of 20, he became one of the most famous and influential[6] British writers. His stories are about people's reactions to extreme[7] situations, and for many of them he used his experiences at sea.

He died in 1924 at his house in Kent, probably of a heart attack[8].

---

1 intellectual [ˌɪntḷˈɛktʃʊəl] (n.) 知識分子
2 reunification [ˌjunəfəˈkeʃn̩] (n.) 統一
3 merchant navy 商船
4 suffer from . . . 飽受⋯⋯之苦
5 clinical depression 憂鬱症
6 influential [ˌɪnflʊˈɛnʃəl] (a.) 有影響力的
7 extreme [ɪkˈstrim] (a.) 極端的
8 heart attack 心臟病發;心肌梗塞

The Secret Agent is set in London. It tells the story of Mr. Verloc, a man who lives a double life: one as the owner of a shop where he sells all sorts of junk[1], and the other as a spy for a foreign government. He lives in a house above his shop with his young wife Winnie, her mother and her brother Stevie, a young man in his early twenties who has a learning disability[2]. There are also a group of anarchists[3], at least one terrorist[4], two police officials and some government officials in the plot.

The idea for this story came from a real event: in 1894 a French anarchist, Martial Bourdin, blew himself up[5] in Greenwich Park, near the Greenwich Royal Observatory[6], when the bomb he was carrying exploded[7]. Everything about this event remained a mystery: it was impossible to discover the reason for the attack, the aim, or even what happened exactly. But although he had very little information, Conrad managed to base a whole novel on this unexplained and violent death.

The Secret Agent was published in 1907, but its themes are so modern that they are often in today's news: terrorism, espionage[8] and power. Conrad shows us the thinking behind terrorism and what terrorists and people in power want to achieve through it. *The Secret Agent* is a spy story, a detective[9] story and a psychological[10] drama.

---

1 junk [dʒʌŋk] (n.) 廢棄的舊物
2 disability [ˌdɪsəˈbɪlətɪ] (n.) 殘障；失能
3 anarchist [ˈænəˌkɪst] (n.) 無政府主義者
4 terrorist [ˈtɛrərɪst] (n.) 恐怖分子
5 blow up 炸毀
6 Greenwich Royal Observatory 格林威治皇家天文台
7 explode [ɪkˈsplod] (v.) 爆炸
8 espionage [ˈɛspɪənɑʒ] (n.) 間諜活動
9 detective [dɪˈtɛktɪv] (a.) 偵探的
10 psychological [ˌsaɪkəˈlɑdʒɪkl] (a.) 心理的

REAL LIFE SECRET AGENTS
Oliver "the Spy" and the Pentrich Revolution

Britain became a parliamentary democracy[1] in 1215, but in 1817 less than 3% of the people had the right to vote[2]. In 1775 thirteen American colonies[3] started a War of Independence from Britain with the idea of creating the first truly democratic country. And in 1789 the French Revolution abolished[4] the monarchy and created a republic. The British workers read about this in newspapers and were not happy.

This situation was made worse by a series of poor crops[5] and a new tax on imported[6] grains[7] that made food very expensive.

In order to vote in 1817 you
needed to tick these 3 boxes:

☐ Male
☐ Over 21
☐ Own property of value

The government knew that political groups were
forming and asking for a change in the law to give
workers the right to vote. So it created a network of
spies and informers to infiltrate[8] these groups and
give the government information. The government
needed an excuse to stop these groups and they were
going to make sure they had one.

1 parliamentary democracy 議會民主制
2 vote [vot] (v.) 投票
3 colony [ˋkɑlənɪ] (n.) 殖民地
4 abolish [əˋbɑlɪʃ] (v.) 廢除
5 crops [krɑps] (n.) 〔複〕作物
6 imported [ɪmˋportɪd] (a.) 進口的
7 grain [gren] (n.) 穀物
8 infiltrate [ɪnˋfɪltret] (v.) 滲透

Oliver the Spy

William J. Oliver, known as "Oliver the Spy", infiltrated a group of workers in Derbyshire, in the north of England. He gave information to the government, and he created the excuse that the government needed. He told the men that people in larger cities like Manchester were angry, and that armed workers were getting ready to march[1] to London to force the government to give them the right to vote.

On 9th June 1817 about 300 men left the village of Pentrich, 14 miles north of Nottingham. They marched south towards London. When they reached the village of Eastwood they realized it was a trap[2]: the soldiers were

When you read _The Secret Agent_

Are there any similarities between the story and the Pentrich Revolution?

Find out more

What was the Peterloo Massacre?

What was the Chartist Movement?

When did women get the right to vote at 21?

When did all men and women get the right to vote at 18?

waiting for them. The men tried to escape but 46 of them were arrested for High Treason[3].

The government wanted to teach the workers a lesson, so the sentences[4] were very hard: death for three men and deportation[5] to Australia and prison for 23 others. None of them ever came back. Their families were forced to leave their homes. Oliver "the Spy" went to work in South Africa.

In 1918, after many small reforms, all men above the age of 21 and all women above the age of 30 got the right to vote.

1　march [mɑrtʃ] (v.) 遊行示威
2　trap [træp] (n.) 陷阱；圈套
3　High Treason 叛國罪；叛逆罪
4　sentence [ˋsɛntəns] (n.) 判決
5　deportation [ˌdɪporˋteʃən] (n.) 驅逐出境

REAL LIFE SECRET AGENTS
The Cambridge Spies

The Cambridge Spies were a group of four men who met at Cambridge University in the 1930s and became secret agents for the Soviet Union during World War II and the Cold War period, which followed the war. Their story is the subject of many books and films.

Anthony Blunt

Donald Maclean

Guy Burgess

Harold Philby

Anthony Blunt, who was a little older than the other three, was teaching at Cambridge and he recruited[1] **Harold "Kim" Philby**, **Donald Maclean** and **Guy Burgess**. A Russian spy who later defected[2] to the UK said there was at least one more spy in the group, but he has never been found.

The four spies were not discovered for a long time. One of the reasons for this was that they came from privileged[3] backgrounds: the British establishment[4] could not even imagine that men from rich families and with a Cambridge University degree could betray[5] their country and be secret agents for the Soviet Union.

After they left Cambridge, they all had important jobs: Anthony Blunt worked for **MI5** during WWII, then became an important art historian, worked for the queen and was knighted[6] in 1956. Guy Burgess became a journalist, worked for the BBC and then for **MI6**. Donald Maclean worked at the Foreign Office. Philby worked in Vienna during the war, helping refugees[7] from Nazi Germany; then he became a journalist, working for various papers including *The Times*, and joined MI6.

1 recruit [rɪˋkrut] (v.) 招收新成員
2 defect [dɪˋfɛkt] (v.) 叛逃
3 privileged [ˋprɪvl̩ɪdʒɪd] (a.) 特權的
4 establishment [ɪsˋtæblɪʃmənt] (n.) 當局
5 betray [bɪˋtre] (v.) 背叛；出賣
6 knight [naɪt] (v.) 封為爵士
7 refugee [͵rɛfjʊˋdʒi] (n.) 難民；流亡者

At MI6 Philby, a Soviet agent, became the head of the anti-Soviet section, and later chief British intelligence[1] officer in the United States. His position at MI6 meant that he could not only pass information to the **KGB** (the Soviet secret services), but he could also make sure that he and the other Cambridge Spies were not discovered. So when MI6 realized there could be a spy inside the Foreign Office, Philby was one of the first to know that Burgess and Maclean were suspects[2]. He told them, and helped them defect to the Soviet Union.

However, after this he also became a suspect and had to resign. Not long after that he, too, defected to the Soviet Union. All three lived there until the end of their lives.

In 1963 the British government discovered that Anthony Blunt was a spy. They offered him immunity[3] in exchange for information. He gave them very little, but he didn't go to prison and kept living in London.

THE BRITISH SECRET SERVICES

MI5 is the domestic[4] intelligence agency[5] that tries to stop possible terrorist attacks and espionage within the UK. It is controlled by the Home Secretary.

MI6 is the foreign intelligence agency. It is controlled by the Foreign Secretary. All MI6 directors since 1909 have signed documents simply with the letter C, to hide their name.

1   intelligence [ɪnˋtɛlədʒəns] (n.) 情報機關
2   suspect [ˋsʌspɛkt] (n.) 可疑分子
3   immunity [ɪˋmjunətɪ] (n.) 豁免
4   domestic [dəˋmɛstɪk] (a.) 國家的
5   agency [ˋedʒənsɪ] (n.) 機構

The Secret Agent

Winnie Verloc

Mr. Verloc

Winnie's Mother

Stevie

Wurmt

Vladimir

Sir Ethel

Chief
Inspector Heat

The Assistant
Commissioner

The Professor

Ossipon

Michaelis

Karl Yundt

1 Match the pictures to the characters.

_____ ① Mrs. Winnie Verloc was young and attractive and looked after her brother.

_____ ② Stevie had fair hair, loved his sister very much and got easily lost.

_____ ③ Winnie's mother's husband was dead and her health wasn't very good.

_____ ④ Mr. Verloc was lazy and fat and had dark hair.

2 Who do you think is most important?
Talk with a friend and decide.

Assistant Commissioner

Police Officer

Home Secretary

Chief Inspector Heat

3 Match the places on the map A–D with the pictures. Use the internet to help you. How many other places can you add to the map?

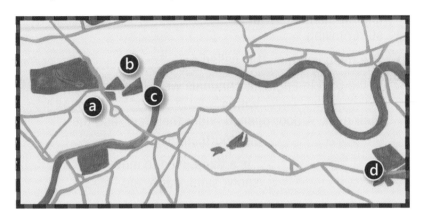

_____ ① The Royal Observatory is in Greenwich Park.

_____ ② Mr. Verloc's house is in Brett Street, in Soho.

_____ ③ There's an important Embassy in Belgravia.

_____ ④ The British Parliament is in the Palace of Westminster on the River Thames.

4 Match the following elements of the story with the places in Exercise 3.

_____ ① the Home Secretary

_____ ② the First Secretary of the Ambassador

_____ ③ the First Meridian

_____ ④ Mrs. Winnie Verloc

5 Look at the pictures and complete the definitions.

a) In the past, a _____ was a vehicle pulled by a horse and used as a taxi. The driver sat on the box and hit the horse with a _____ to make it start moving.

b) The thing you aim at is called a _____ .

c) In the past in England, criminals were hanged from the _____ , with a _____ around their neck. A door opened under their feet, and the _____ was fourteen feet.

d) A _____ is a thing used to move _____ , snow, sand, earth, etc.

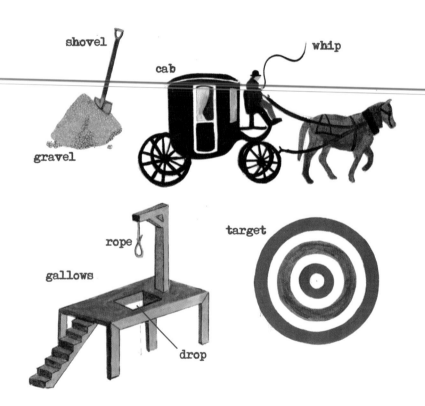

shovel

cab

whip

gravel

rope

gallows

target

drop

6 Read the text and match the words in bold to their definition.

When there is a crime, the police need to investigate and discover who committed it. If they have a suspect, they need to find evidence that incriminates him or her. Sometimes if the suspect feels guilt, he or she confesses, which usually makes things easier for the police. If there is enough evidence, they arrest the person and they put him or her on trial. If it is clear during the trial that the suspect is guilty, the judge decides the sentence. In Britain the law says that the sentence cannot be death, so if the crime is serious, the sentence is usually a certain amount of time in prison. But in the past the death penalty was legal. Executions were carried out in prisons, often by hanging from the gallows with a rope around their neck. Today if a prisoner behaves well in prison, he or she can be released before the end of their sentence on parole, and live out of prison. However, if they commit even a small crime, they have to go back to prison and finish their sentence.

a ——————: allowed by the law.
b ——————: the legal process to decide if someone committed a crime.
c ——————: something that proves something else.
d ——————: allowed to leave prison.
e ——————: did something that is considered wrong.
f ——————: a wooden construction for hanging people in executions.
g ——————: someone the police think has committed a crime.
h ——————: try to prove what happened and who did something.
i ——————: when someone feels very bad for something they have done.
j ——————: permission to leave prison if the prisoner promises to behave well.
k ——————: admits they have done something wrong.
l ——————: the way the criminal will be punished.
m ——————: killings of people sentenced to death .
n ——————: makes someone seem like they have committed a crime.
o ——————: a very thick string.

1. Mr. Verloc

🎧 1 When Mr. Verloc went out, he often left Stevie, his brother-in-law[1], to look after his shop. And his wife, Mrs. Verloc, to look after Stevie. The shop was small, and so was the house above it. It was like a square box in Brett Street. The shop window showed cheap dusty items. The customers looked generally as if they didn't have much money.

There was a bell above the door and when it rang, Mr. Verloc came from the sitting room at the back of the shop. He was overweight[2], had dark hair, heavy eyelids and an air of[3] having spent the day fully dressed[4] on an unmade bed. He then sold his customer some object at a price that was clearly too high.

Sometimes it was Mrs. Verloc who appeared when the shop bell rang. Mrs. Winnie Verloc was a young, attractive woman who seemed very uninterested in the customers in the shop and the special visitors who went into the sitting room at the back. The door of the shop was the only entrance[5] to the house.

Winnie's mother also lived with them. She was a heavy woman, with swollen[6] legs that made her disabled, and she was a widow[7]. In the past she had a lodging house[8] where Winnie helped her look after the lodgers[9], and that's where she met Mr. Verloc. He stayed there every time he returned from his frequent mysterious trips to Europe.

---

1 brother-in-law 小舅子
2 overweight [ˋovɚˏwet] (a.) 體重超重的
3 an air of 帶著……樣子
4 fully dressed 穿戴整齊
5 entrance [ˋɛntrəns] (n.) 入口
6 swollen [ˋswolən] (a.) 浮腫的
7 widow [ˋwɪdo] (n.) 寡婦
8 lodging house 供臨時住宿的租屋
9 lodger [ˋlɑdʒɚ] (n.) 租宿者

When they got married, Winnie's mother sold the lodging house because it wasn't convenient[1] for Mr. Verloc's other business. What his business was he did not say. His work was in a way political, he told Winnie once. It was impossible for Winnie's mother to discover anything more.

The couple took Winnie's mother and brother to their new home. Winnie was very fond of her delicate[2] brother, and Mr. Verloc was kind and generous, so Winnie's mother felt that the poor boy was safe in this hard world.

Winnie's brother, Stevie, was 23 years old, of slight[3] build[4], with fair hair, and difficult to look after. He could read and write, but as an errand[5] boy he was not a great success. He forgot his messages; he was easily distracted[6] by street cats and dogs and he got lost. When something confused him, he stuttered[7]. He helped his sister with blind love in her household[8] work. Winnie looked after him like a mother.

Such was the house, the household, and the business that Mr. Verloc left behind him on his way towards Hyde Park at half-past ten on that particular morning.

Mr. Verloc

- Who is in Mr. Verloc's household?
- What jobs does Mr. Verloc do?

---

1 convenient [kən'vinjənt] (a.) 方便的
2 delicate ['dɛləkət] (a.) 棘手的
3 slight [slaɪt] (a.) 瘦小的
4 build [bɪld] (n.) 體格
5 errand ['ɛrənd] (n.) 差事
6 distract [dɪ'strækt] (v.) 使分心
7 stutter ['stʌtɚ] (v.) 結巴；口吃
8 household ['haʊsˌhold] (a.) 家庭的

2. The Embassy

Half-past ten in the morning was unusually early for Mr. Verloc. He watched the busy streets, pleased to notice the signs of the city's wealth and luxury [1]. All these people needed to be protected. Protection is the first necessity of wealth and luxury.

He was a lazy man. Or maybe he believed that nothing people do, has ever any effect. He also had an air which people who work never have. The air that is common to men who make money from the weaknesses, the stupidity or the lowest fears of people.

He had some business with an Embassy [2]. A letter ordering him to be there that morning was in his pocket. When he arrived, he was taken into a small room with a heavy writing-table and a few chairs. Mr. Wurmt, an official from the Embassy, walked in holding some papers. Mr. Verloc recognized his own handwriting.

"I have here some of your reports," said Mr. Wurmt. "We are not very satisfied with the attitude [3] of the police in this country. They are too soft. We need an event which will attract the attention of the police and make judges give harder sentences. Something that will increase the tension [4] which undoubtedly exists . . ."

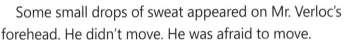

"There's a dangerous level of tension," said Mr. Verloc interrupting him. "My reports for the last twelve months make that very clear."

"I have read your reports," Mr. Wurmt said. "They are useless."

There was silence. Then Mr. Wurmt spoke.

"You are too fat," he said. "I think that you should see Mr. Vladimir. Please wait here," and he left the room.

Some small drops of sweat appeared on Mr. Verloc's forehead. He didn't move. He was afraid to move.

A servant came and took him to the first floor, opened a door and let him in. The room was large, with three windows. A young man with a big face was sitting in a large armchair in front of a large wooden writing table. He spoke in French to Mr. Wurmt, who was leaving, and said: "You're quite right, my dear. He's fat—the animal."

Mr. Vladimir, First Secretary of the Ambassador[5], was a favorite in high society. "You understand French, I suppose?" he said.

---

1. luxury ['lʌkʃərɪ] (n.) 奢華
2. Embassy ['ɛmbəsɪ] (n.) 大使館
3. attitude ['ætətjud] (n.) 態度
4. tension ['tɛnʃən] (n.) 緊張局勢
5. ambassador [æm'bæsədə] (n.) 大使；使節

Mr. Verloc said that he did and muttered[1] something about his service in the French army. Suddenly Mr. Vladimir began to speak in English with no sign of a foreign accent[2].

"How long have you worked for the Embassy here?" he asked.

"Eleven years, ever since the time of the late[3] Baron Stott-Wartenheim," Mr. Verloc answered.

"Baron Stott-Wartenheim was a gullible[4] old man. Things are different now. So, tell me, why did you let yourself get out of condition like this? Look at yourself. You—a member of the hungry proletariat[5]? You—a desperate socialist[6] or anarchist . . . which is it?"

"Anarchist," said Mr. Verloc.

"Do you really think anybody will believe you?" continued Mr. Vladimir. "Not even the stupid will, and they are all stupid. You are simply ridiculous, not very smart, and lazy. As far as I can judge from our documents, you have done nothing to earn your money for the last three years."

"Nothing?" exclaimed[7] Verloc. "I have several times prevented . . ."

---

1 mutter [ˈmʌtɚ] (v.) 低聲嘀咕
2 accent [ˈæksɛnt] (n.) 口音；腔調
3 late [let] (a.) 已故的
4 gullible [ˈgʌləbl̩] (a.) 易受騙的

5 proletariat [ˌprolə'tɛriət] (n.) 無產階級；勞工階級
6 socialist [ˈsoʃəlɪst] (n.) 社會主義者
7 exclaim [ɪksˈklem] (v.) 叫喊著說出

"The idea that preventing[1] is better than curing[2]," interrupted Mr. Vladimir, "is stupid in a general way, but in this particular case it's more than stupid. The evil is already here. We don't want to prevent—we want to cure. I'm in charge now, and I tell you clearly that you will have to earn your money. No work, no pay."

Mr. Verloc was surprised and started to feel afraid.

"We want something that will cause repression[3]," said Mr. Vladimir. "England is silly with its respect for individual freedom. I have an idea."

Mr. Vladimir explained his idea showing himself to know very little about the revolutionary world, which shocked the silent Mr. Verloc.

"We want the middle class to feel fear, and we need a series of outrages[4] to do that," Mr. Vladimir said. "These outrages don't need to be especially violent, but they must be very worrying. They should be directed against buildings. What is the latest fashion in middle class beliefs[5], Mr. Verloc?"

Mr. Verloc moved his shoulders slightly[6].

"You are too lazy to think," said Mr. Vladimir. "Listen carefully. These days the middle class believes neither in royalty[7] nor religion. Therefore the Palace and the Church should not be targeted[8]. The latest fashion is science. To be successful, an attack should make it clear that you are determined to destroy society. Anyone with a good job believes in learning and science. What do you think of an attack on astronomy[9]?"

(7) Mr. Verloc thought this idea was stupid.

"The whole civilized world has heard of Greenwich," continued Mr. Vladimir, very proud of himself. "The first meridian[10] is the perfect target."

Mr. Verloc didn't know what to say.

"You may go now," said Mr. Vladimir. "We want a dynamite[11] outrage. I give you a month, or your connection with us will end."

Mr. Vladimir

- What do you think of his ideas?
- What kind of person do you think he is?
- Can you think of any people like this today in your country?

1 prevent [prɪˋvɛnt] (v.) 預防	7 royalty [ˋrɔɪəltɪ] (n.) (總稱) 皇族
2 cure [kjʊr] (v.) 治療	8 target [ˋtɑrgɪt] (v.) 以……為目標
3 repression [rɪˋprɛʃən] (n.) 鎮壓	9 astronomy [əsˋtrɑnəmɪ] (n.) 天文學
4 outrage [ˋaʊt͵redʒ] (n.) 憤慨	10 first meridian 西經一度線
5 belief [bɪˋlif] (n.) 信仰；信念	(指格林威治皇家天文台)
6 slightly [ˋslaɪtlɪ] (adv.) 稍微	11 dynamite [ˋdaɪnə͵maɪt] (a.) 具爆炸性的

3. The Meeting

A few days later, Mr. Verloc's political group met in the sitting room at the back of the shop in Brett Street.

Michaelis was speaking, but he was very fat and speaking was difficult. After 15 years in prison he was now out on parole[1] and had an enormous stomach and face. When he was in prison he formed a vision[2] of a fair society, and as usual he was talking about it in very unclear but passionate[3] words.

On the other side of the room, Karl Yundt giggled[4] with a toothless mouth. The Terrorist, as he called himself, was old and bald[5], with an extraordinary[6] expression[7] of hatred in his dead eyes.

"I've always dreamt," he said, "of a group of men who are strong enough to kill and die in the service of humanity[8]. That's my dream."

Michaelis was still speaking. He always thought aloud inside the four walls of his lonely prison cell. He was no good in discussion because hearing another voice confused his thoughts. So he paid no attention to the others and kept talking.

The room was getting very hot, and Mr. Verloc opened the door leading into the kitchen. This showed Stevie, who was sitting very good and quiet at the table, drawing circles[9], circles, circles; always circles.

(9)   Alexander Ossipon, also called the Doctor, an ex-medical student without a degree, went to look over Stevie's shoulder. Then he came back, and talking like an expert he said, "Very good. Very characteristic[10] perfectly typical of this form of degeneracy[11]—these drawings, I mean."

"Do you think it's right to call that young man a degenerate?" muttered Mr. Verloc.

"Yes, that's what he may be called scientifically," Ossipon replied. "It's enough to look at the shape of his ears. If you read Lombroso[12] . . ."

Karl Yundt interrupted Ossipon.

"Lombroso is stupid. For him the criminal[13] is the prisoner. What about those who put him there? And what is crime? Does he know that? He is a fool who has made money by looking at the ears and the teeth of a lot of poor, unlucky people. Do teeth and ears mark a criminal? And what about the law that marks him even better? The law is a red-hot branding instrument[14] invented by those who have too much food to protect themselves against the hungry. Can't you smell and hear the skin of the people burn? That's how criminals are made."

---

1 parole [pə`rol] (n.) 假釋

2 vision [`vɪʒən] (n.) 憧憬

3 passionate [`pæʃənɪt] (a.) 激昂的

4 giggle [`gɪgl] (v.) 咯咯地笑

5 bald [bɔld] (a.) 禿頭的

6 extraordinary [ɪk`strɔrdn͵ɛrɪ] (a.) 特別的

7 expression [ɪk`sprɛʃən] (n.) 神情

8 humanity [hju`mænətɪ] (n.) 人道

9 circle [`sɝkl] (n.) 圓圈

10 characteristic [͵kærəktə`rɪstɪk] (a.) 特有的

11 degeneracy [dɪ`dʒɛnərəsɪ] (n.) 退化

12 Cesare Lombroso (1835-1909)：義大利犯罪學家、精神病學家，刑事人類學派的創始人

13 criminal [`krɪmənl] (n.) 罪犯

14 branding instrument 烙印器具

(10) However, Karl Yundt, the famous Terrorist, was all talk[1]. He was no man of action; he was not even a good public speaker.

Stevie got up from the table and was leaving the kitchen when he heard Karl Yundt's words. In shock, he dropped his drawing and stared[2] with frightened eyes at the old terrorist. Stevie knew very well that hot iron applied to one's skin hurts very much. His mouth dropped open.

"Do you know," said Karl Yundt, "how I describe present economic conditions? They are cannibalistic[3]. That's what they are! They are feeding their greed[4] on the flesh[5] and the warm blood of the people."

Stevie's eyes became even bigger and more frightened.

Soon after that, the meeting ended and the men left.

Mr. Verloc was not satisfied with his friends. In the light of Mr. Vladimir's ideas about outrages they were useless. But the shop wasn't doing very well, and he needed the Embassy money.

Jobs

- What is Mr. Verloc's main job? What is his second job? Why does he need two jobs?
- How many people do you know who have more than one job?

---

1 all talk 光說不練
2 stare [stɛr] (v.) 盯；凝視
3 cannibalistic [ˌkænəbḷˈɪstɪk]
   (a.) 食人肉的
4 greed [grid] (n.) 貪婪
5 flesh [flɛʃ] (n.) 肉

(11) When Mr. Verloc closed the door, he realized that Stevie was still in the kitchen. He was surprised to see him there. He didn't know what to say to him, so he didn't say anything and simply left him there.

Winnie was asleep, and he woke her up. "Stevie is downstairs. I don't know what to do with him," he said.

She got up immediately and went into the kitchen. She came back a bit later, and said that Stevie was very agitated[1].

"That boy hears too much of what you talk about. He was shouting and crying about something he overheard[2] about eating people's flesh and drinking blood. He shouldn't hear what your friends say. He believes it's all true and becomes very upset[3]."

Mr. Verloc made no comment.

Stevie

- Why does Stevie believe everything is true?
- Do you sometimes hear what other people are saying and not understand it?

4. The Professor

A few days later, Ossipon was sitting at one of the little tables in the Silenus Restaurant early in the afternoon. He was trying to make conversation with a small man with glasses and old, dirty clothes. The small man, known as the Professor, didn't seem interested in talking to him, and this made Ossipon uncomfortable.

"Been sitting here long?" asked Ossipon.

"An hour or more."

"Then maybe you haven't heard the news. Have you?"

The little man shook his head, but showed no curiosity.

"Do you give your stuff[4] to anybody who asks you for it?" asked Ossipon.

"I never say no."

"But what if a spy from the police asked you for your wares[5]? Then they could arrest you with the proof[6] in their hands."

"Proof of what? Dealing in[7] explosives[8] without a license[9]? I don't think they want to arrest me. I know they don't."

"Why?" asked Ossipon.

---

1 agitated [ˈædʒəˌtetɪd] (a.) 激動的
2 overhear [ˌovəˈhɪr] (v.) 無意中聽到
  （三態：overhear, overheard,
  overheard）
3 upset [ʌpˈsɛt] (a.) 心煩的；不適的
4 stuff [stʌf] (n.) 東西；玩意

5 wares [wɛrz] (n.)〔複〕貨物
6 proof [pruf] (n.) 證據
7 deal in sth 賣某物
8 explosive [ɪkˈsplosɪv] (n.) 爆炸物
9 license [ˈlaɪsn̩s] (n.) 執照

"Because they know very well I always carry some of my wares on me." He touched the front of his coat. "I will never be arrested. Policemen aren't heroes."

"They don't need to be," Ossipon replied. "They only need to find a policeman who does not know you carry enough explosives in your pocket to blow yourself and a lot of other people to pieces."

"I've never said that I could not be got rid of[1]. But that's not an arrest. Anyway, they know I can detonate[2] the bomb in a few seconds."

Ossipon looked around the restaurant.

"Your bomb is enough to destroy this room and kill everybody in it."

"You need to have a very strong character," the small man continued, "and very few people have it. The police know that I have it. They know that I am not afraid of dying nor of killing a lot of people. That's what makes me stronger and better than them."

"There are individuals of character in the police, too," said Ossipon.

"Maybe. But their character is built on middle-class morality[3]. Mine is free from anything like that. They have to consider life, and life is complicated[4] and open to attack. But I only have to consider death, which is simple and cannot be attacked. So I'm stronger and better than anybody else."

1 be got rid of 這裡指被殺死
2 detonate [ˈdɛtəˌnet] (v.) 使爆炸
3 morality [məˈrælətɪ] (n.) 道德
4 complicated [ˈkɑmpləˌketɪd] (a.) 複雜的

"I am afraid I have to spoil[1] that thought for you," said Ossipon. "A man blew himself up in Greenwich Park this morning."

Ossipon pulled a newspaper out of his pocket.

"Here it is. Bomb in Greenwich Park. There isn't much so far. Half-past eleven. Foggy morning. Enormous hole in the ground under a tree. All around fragments[2] of a man's body blown to pieces. I don't understand the purpose[3] of it. It may have negative results for us."

There was a silence, then Ossipon spoke again.

"You've given a bomb to someone recently, haven't you? The day the police learn how to do their job, they will shoot you on sight[4], before you can detonate your wares."

"Yes," the little man agreed. "But isn't that exactly what we want? We want them to forget their own rules and principles[5] of legality[6]. I will be very pleased when the police start shooting us in the streets and the public is happy. That will be when their morality starts to disintegrate[7]. That will be the beginning of our victory. That is what we should try to achieve."

"But was it one of your bombs that exploded this morning?" asked Ossipon. "We in the London group had no knowledge. Can you describe the person you gave the stuff to?"

"Yes, with one word: Verloc."

(15) Ossipon sat back on his chair, shocked.
"Verloc! Impossible."

Bomb

- Who is responsible for the bomb?
- How do we know this?
- Where did the bomb explode?
- Who was killed?

"He was an important member of the group, as far as I understand."

"Yes," said Ossipon. "Important. No, not exactly. More useful than important. A man of no ideas. Intellectually a nobody. His only talent was his ability to escape the attention of the police. He was married. Did he give you any idea of his intentions?"

---

1 spoil [spɔɪl] (v.) 打破
2 fragment [ˈfrægmənt] (n.) 碎片
3 purpose [ˈpɝpəs] (n.) 目的
4 on sight 一見到立即
5 principle [ˈprɪnsəpl] (n.) 原則
6 legality [lɪˈgælətɪ] (n.) 合法 (性)
7 disintegrate [dɪsˈɪntəgret] (v.) 使瓦解

"He told me it was for a demonstration against a building," said the Professor.

"What do you think happened?" asked Ossipon.

I don't know. The timer was set for twenty minutes after he switched on the detonator[1]. If you want a bomb to explode earlier, you only need to give it a sharp shock. So he either waited too long, or he accidentally dropped the bomb. Only a fool could do something like that."

Ossipon sat in his chair thinking. Verloc's shop might already be a police trap, so he didn't really want to go there. But if the man in the park was in pieces as the newspapers said, maybe he was impossible to identify[2]. So perhaps the police had no special reason for watching Verloc's shop.

"I wonder what I should do now," Ossipon muttered.

"Get as much as you can from his wife. There must be money somewhere," said the Professor.

Ossipon

- **What is he going to do now?**

1 detonator [ˈdɛtə.netɚ] (n.) 引爆裝置
2 identify [aɪˈdɛntə.faɪ] (v.) 識別
3 appetite [ˈæpə.taɪt] (n.) 食欲
4 mangle [ˈmæŋgl̩] (v.) 使受嚴重損傷
5 remains [rɪˈmenz] (n.)〔複〕遺骸
6 sheet [ʃit] (n.) 一塊（布）
7 leftovers [ˈleft.ovɚz] (n.)〔複〕吃剩的飯菜
8 tin can 錫罐
9 shovel [ˈʃʌvl̩] (n.) 鏟子

5. Chief Inspector Heat

(17) Chief Inspector Heat was having a bad day. First of all, his department received a telegram from Greenwich that morning. "Just my luck," he thought. "Less than a week after I told the Home Secretary that there was absolutely no anarchist activity in London."

Plus he was hungry, and he had to examine a body at the hospital. As soon as he got to the hospital, he lost his appetite[3]. He was not used to examining closely the mangled[4] remains[5] of human beings. He was shocked when another police officer lifted the sheet[6] from the body. There were pieces of clothes, burnt and covered in blood, mixed with what looked like the leftovers[7] of a lion's meal. He didn't manage to eat anything for the rest of the day.

"He's all there. Every bit of him," said a police officer. The officer told him his story. "I was the first to arrive after the explosion," he explained. "The old woman I spoke to said she saw two men coming out of the station. She couldn't tell if they were together. She said one was overweight and the other was fair and slight and he was carrying a bright tin can[8] in one hand. And, here he is. Fair. Slight. Look at that foot there. I picked up the legs first, one after the other. There were pieces of him everywhere. We had to use a shovel[9]."

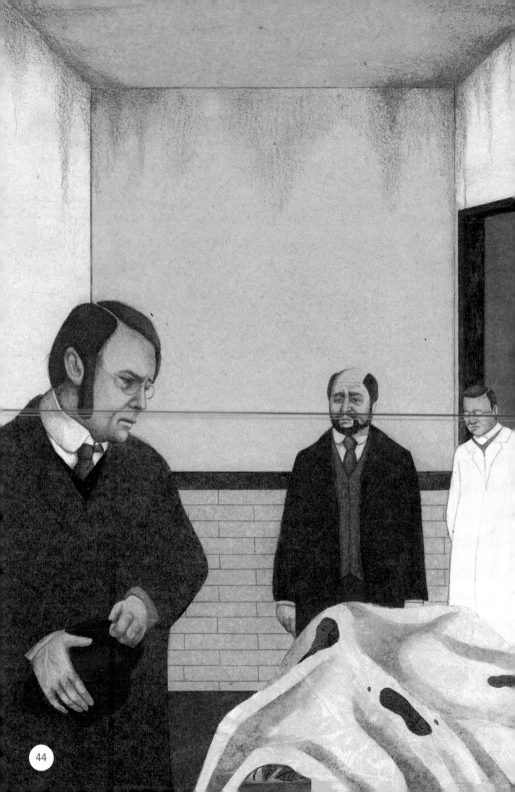

18 The officer paused. "He probably stumbled[1] against the root of a tree and fell," he said, "and that thing he was carrying exploded right under his chest."

Chief Inspector Heat overcame[2] his physical disgust[3] and put out his hand and took up the least bloody of the pieces. It was a narrow strip of velvet[4] with a large triangular[5] piece of dark blue cloth hanging from it.

"The old woman noticed the velvet collar," said the officer. "Dark blue overcoat with a velvet collar, she told us."

The Chief Inspector moved to one of the windows to examine the piece of blue cloth. With a quick movement he took it off the velvet, put it into his pocket, turned round and put the velvet collar back on the table.

"Cover up," he said to one of the officers, and left quickly.

At the office the Chief Inspector went straight into the Assistant Commissioner's room.

Explosion

- Who was carrying the bomb?
- What happened to him?
- Underline the words in the story that tell us.

---

1 stumble [ˈstʌmbl̩] (v.) 絆倒
2 overcome [ˌovəˈkʌm] (v.) 克服
   （三態：overcome, overcame, overcome）
3 disgust [dɪsˈgʌst] (n.) 作嘔
4 velvet [ˈvɛlvɪt] (n.) 天鵝絨
5 triangular [traɪˈæŋgjələ] (a.) 三角形的

45

"You were right," said the Assistant Commissioner. "The reports have come in, and we know where every London anarchist is. They didn't commit[1] this crime and they had nothing to do with it."

Then the Chief Inspector told him the story and his conclusions[2] so far.

"In my opinion," he said, "the two men arrived together and they went in different directions when they were about a hundred yards from the Observatory walls. The fog, though not very thick, probably helped the bigger man get out of the park without being noticed. It looks like he took the smaller man to the spot[3], and then left him there to do the job on his own.

"Are you trying to find the bigger man?" the Assistant Commissioner asked.

The Chief Inspector mentioned the name of a station. "That's where they came from, sir," he said. "The porter[4] who took the tickets at Maze Hill remembers two men matching the description. The big man got out of a third-class compartment[5] with a bright tin can in his hand. On the platform he gave it to the fair-haired[6] young man who was following him. All this matches exactly what the old woman told the police officer in Greenwich."

（20）　The Assistant Commissioner thought these two men had nothing to do with the attack. It was only an old woman telling a story.

　"There were lots of bits of tin can," said the Chief Inspector. "That's a good connection."

　"And these men came from that little country station," the Assistant Commissioner continued. "Two foreign anarchists coming from that place. It's rather unlikely."

　"Yes, sir. But Michaelis is staying in a cottage in that area."

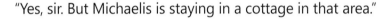

1　commit [kə`mɪt] (v.) 犯 ((罪)
2　conclusion [kən`kluʒən] (n.) 推論
3　spot [spɑt] (n.) 地點
4　porter [`portɚ] (n.) 行李員
5　compartment [kəm`pɑrtmənt] (n.) 車廂
6　fair-haired [`fɛr`hɛrd] (a.) 金髮的

6. Michaelis

(21)   After Michaelis was released[1] from prison, a rich old lady decided to help him, and she gave him a cottage she owned in the countryside. This lady was one of the most influential and important connections of the Assistant Commissioner's wife.

Michaelis's sentence was life in prison for complicity[2] after he and some others tried to rescue[3] prisoners from a police van. A policeman was accidentally killed. The policeman left a wife and three small children, and the public was shocked. Michaelis, young and slim, had nothing to do with the killing, but when he spoke at his trial[4] he said: "the death of the policeman makes me really sad. I'm also sorry we didn't manage to rescue the prisoners. That makes me sad, too."

So the public hated him, and when he was released on parole after 15 years he was in all the newspapers.

One evening Michaelis was taken to the great lady's house by an important guest. Although he could not explain any of his great ideas about social justice, he impressed[5] the great lady with his passion and his optimism[6]. She didn't think he was dangerous, and she decided to look after him.

---

1 release [rɪˋlis] (v.) 釋放
2 complicity [kəmˋplɪsətɪ] (n.) 共謀
3 rescue [ˋrɛskju] (v.) 救援
4 trial [ˋtraɪəl] (n.) 審問
5 impress [ɪmˋprɛs] (v.) 使印象深刻
6 optimism [ˋɑptəmɪzəm] (n.) 樂觀

The Assistant Commissioner shared the view of his wife's influential connection that Michaelis was a sentimentalist[1], a little mad, but unable to hurt anyone intentionally. So when the Chief Inspector mentioned his name in connection with the bomb, the Assistant Commissioner realized the danger.

"Michaelis is out on parole," the Assistant Commissioner thought. "If we arrest him, the police will take him back to prison to finish his sentence. He will die in prison smothered[2] by his own fat, and my wife will never forgive me."

"Can you connect Michaelis with this case?" he asked.

"Well, sir," said Chief Inspector Heat, "we have enough information that points in his direction. A man like that shouldn't be free anyway."

"You will want some conclusive evidence[3]," replied the Assistant Commissioner.

"There will be no difficulty in getting enough evidence against him," said Chief Inspector Heat. "You may trust me for that, sir."

The Assistant Commissioner was becoming more and more annoyed. "Heat has a plan against Michaelis, and maybe against me," he thought.

"I have reason to think that when you came into this room," said the Assistant Commissioner, "you were not thinking of Michaelis."

"You have reason to think, sir?" said Chief Inspector Heat.

(23) "Yes," said the Assistant Commissioner; "I have. If Michaelis is really a suspect, why haven't you investigated[4] him already, either personally or by sending one of your men to his village?"

"Do you think, sir, that I haven't done my duty?" the Chief Inspector asked.

"That is not what I meant," replied the Assistant Commissioner with a face that said, "and you know it." "There is no doubt about your ability," he continued, "but what real evidence can you bring against Michaelis? I mean apart from[5] the fact that the two suspects traveled from a railway station within three miles of the village where Michaelis is living now."

"This by itself is enough for us to keep going in that direction, sir, with that type of man," said the Chief Inspector.

"Do you think that Michaelis had anything to do with the preparation of the bomb?" the Assistant Commissioner asked.

"I don't think he did. But it's clear that he is connected with this in some way. He's part of a group which is on our 'dangerous' list."

The Chief Inspector had no doubt that Michaelis knew something about this outrage, but he was certain that he did not know too much. Probably less than, for example, the Professor. It was impossible to arrest the Professor without breaking some rules. But the rules of the game did not protect Michaelis.

---

1 sentimentalist [ˌsɛntəˈmɛntl̩ɪst] (n.) 多愁善感的人
2 smother [ˈsmʌðɚ] (v.) 使窒息
3 evidence [ˈɛvədəns] (n.) 證據
4 investigate [ɪnˈvɛstəˌget] (v.) 調查；研究
5 apart from 除……之外

Rules of the Game

- What is the game? And what are the rules? Discuss with a friend.

"Tell me what you discovered in Greenwich, Chief Inspector."

"I have an address," said the Chief Inspector, pulling out of his pocket a piece of dark blue cloth with "32 Brett Street" written on it in ink. "This belongs to the overcoat the dead man was wearing. Of course, we don't know if the overcoat was his. It's the address of a shop, and the owner of the shop is Mr. Verloc."

The two men looked at each other.

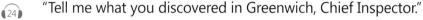

"Of course," continued the Chief Inspector, "the department has no official documents about Verloc. He is my private informer. A friend of mine in the French police told me that he was an Embassy spy."

"I see. Well then, how long have you been in private touch with this Embassy spy?"

"I saw him for the first time a little more than seven years ago, when two Imperial Highnesses[1] and the Imperial Chancellor[2] were on a visit here. The man gave me a piece of very serious information about a possible attack on the Imperial Highnesses."

"What did you do next?" asked the Assistant Commissioner.

(25) "I went into his shop one evening. He said that he was married, and that all he wanted was to continue with his little business. His business is not entirely legal, so I promised him that, as long as he didn't do anything too criminal, the police were happy to leave him alone."

"What do you get from him in exchange for your protection?"

"Information. I send him a short message, unsigned[3], and he answers me in the same way at my private address. My opinion is that he knows nothing of this affair[4]."

"How can you explain this?" said the Assistant Commissioner pointing at the piece of cloth with Verloc's address.

"I can't. It can't be explained by what I know, not at this present moment. I think that the man who had most to do with it is Michaelis."

"What about the man who escaped from the park?"

"He's probably far away by this time," said the Chief Inspector.

"Find him, Chief Inspector, and meet me early tomorrow morning with information."

As soon as the Chief Inspector left, the Assistant Commissioner also left the building.

---

1 Imperial Highness 皇室成員
2 Imperial Chancellor 財政大臣
3 unsigned [ʌnˈsaɪnd] (a.) 未署名的
4 affair [əˈfɛr] (n.) 情況

The Assistant Commissioner entered a public building and asked to speak with the Home Secretary. He was led into a large room where the enormous Home Secretary, Sir Ethelred, was standing.

"Please tell me if this is the beginning of another dynamite campaign[1]," the Home Secretary said. "Don't go into details. I have no time for that."

"No, I really don't think it is. But there's much in this affair that is not typical of an anarchist outrage, and that's why I am here."

"Very well. Go on[2]. Only no details, please."

The Assistant Commissioner told him what he knew from his conversation with Chief Inspector Heat. "There is something under the surface[3] of this case that requires special attention."

"What is your general idea? Be brief. No need to give details."

"Well, I think that secret agents should not be accepted, as they increase the dangers of the evil against which they are used. It is obvious that spies will fabricate[4] information. But in political and revolutionary action the professional spy has every possibility to fabricate the facts themselves. The result is imitation in one direction, and panic[5], hasty laws and blind hate on the other. So this case should be kept secret, and I thought I should talk to you first."

---

1 campaign [kæm`pen] (n.) 一連串攻擊
2 go on 繼續下去 (贊同對方去做某事的說法)
3 surface [`sɝfɪs] (n.) 表面
4 fabricate [`fæbrɪ‚ket] (v.) 杜撰
5 panic [`pænɪk] (n.) 恐慌

(27) "I am glad there's somebody in the police who thinks that the Home Secretary may be trusted now and then. Be as brief as you can."

"I'm not going to give you details, Sir Ethelred. The address on the bomber's overcoat is such an important fact that the explanation for it will go to the bottom of this affair. Instead of instructing Heat to go on with this case, my intention is to try and find this explanation personally—by myself, I mean—at the shop in Brett Street, and from this famous secret agent."

"Why not leave it to Heat?"

"Because he thinks his duty is to send to prison as many famous anarchists as he can even if he hasn't got good evidence, instead of looking into what is below the surface. He's an excellent officer, but this is a special case. Besides, I want a free hand—a freer hand than we should give a normal inspector. I am not going to spare[1] this Verloc. Frightening him will not be very difficult. But he has the explanation. I need your permission[2] to promise him that he will be safe."

Heat

- What does Heat want to do? Why?

28 "Certainly," said the Home Secretary. "Find out as much as you can; find it out in your own way."

"I'll start immediately," said the Assistant Commissioner.

"Report back to me as soon as you can," said the Home Secretary.

The Assistant Commissioner went back to his office to change his clothes and send a note to his wife. They had an invitation to dinner with Michaelis' great lady that evening, so he asked his wife to make his apologies[3] to her. Then he left the office for Brett Street.

Assistant Commissioner

- Who does he think is responsible?
- Who does he not want to be arrested? Why?
- Who is the great lady? Tell a friend.

---

1 spare [spɛr] (v.) 饒恕
2 permission [pəˈmɪʃən] (n.) 許可；同意
3 apology [əˈpɑlədʒɪ] (n.) 道歉

8. Stevie

After insisting with several people who knew her late husband, Mrs. Verloc's mother got a place in an almshouse[1]. The news surprised her daughter.

"What did you want to do that for?" asked her daughter. Winnie preferred not to know all the facts, so before her mother could answer, she asked, "And how did you manage it, Mother?"

"Poor Daddy's friends, my dear," said her mother.

She didn't want to talk about her reasons. She wanted to leave because she knew Mr. Verloc was a good husband, but she didn't know for how long. And she felt that her presence in the house might shorten the duration of his goodness. She also wanted to make Stevie completely dependent on Mr. Verloc, so that he would take care of the poor boy forever. She left her family to make sure that Mr. Verloc paid for her son's future.

When the cab[2] arrived to take her to the almshouse, Winnie's mother was shocked. A very weak and sick horse, slowly pulled a carriage on wobbly[3] wheels. The driver had an iron hook[4] instead of one of his hands. A policeman had to reassure her: "I know the driver," he said, "and in twenty years he's never had an accident."

---

1 almshouse ['ɑmz,haʊs] (n.) 救濟院
2 cab [kæb] (n.) 出租馬車
3 wobbly ['wɑblɪ] (a.) 不穩定的
4 hook [hʊk] (n.) 鉤子

(30) Winnie followed her mother into the cab and Stevie climbed on the box[1]. The journey took a long time because the horse was very slow. Stevie stared at the horse and became increasingly nervous.

"Don't whip[2]," he said at last. "You mustn't," stuttered Stevie. "It hurts."

"Mustn't whip?" said the driver, and he immediately whipped, because he had to earn his money.

But Stevie suddenly got down from the box and caused confusion[3] in the street.

"Stevie! Get up on the box immediately, and don't try to get down again."

"No. No. Walk. Must walk."

Winnie managed to convince him to go back on the box. Finally, they arrived. And Winnie and her mother went into the house. Stevie helped to carry some parcels inside. Then he came out and stared at the poor horse. The cabman walked over to him.

"He isn't lame[4]," said the driver. "He isn't sore[5]. Do you think it's easy to sit behind this horse until three and four o'clock in the morning? Cold and hungry. Looking for fares[6]. Drunks[7]."

Stevie kept looking at the horse.

"I am a night cabby[8]," he said. "I've got a wife and four kids at home. This isn't an easy world."

---

1 box [bɑks] (n.)〔舊〕舊時出租馬車的駕馬區
2 whip [hwɪp] (v.) 鞭打
3 confusion [kənˈfjuʒən] (n.) 困惑
4 lame [lem] (a.) 跛腳的
5 sore [sor] (a.) 疼痛發炎的
6 fare [fɛr] (n.) 車資
7 drunk [drʌŋk] (n.) 酒鬼
8 cabby [ˈkæbɪ] (n.) 出租馬車的駕駛

(31) Stevie's face was twitching[9] and his feelings came out in their usual brief form. "Bad! Bad!"

"Hard on horses, but even harder on poor men like me," the cabby said.

"Poor! Poor!" stuttered out Stevie, pushing his hands deeper into his pockets. He could say nothing. He remembered the times his father hit him and he hid in a dark corner, frightened, sore and miserable. His sister always came along and carried him off to bed with her, into a heaven of consoling[10] peace. He wanted to console the horse and the cabbie the way Winnie always consoled him, but he knew it was impossible.

Winnie left the house and she and Stevie went to take the bus. They saw the horse and the cab parked outside a pub. Winnie recognized it.

"Poor animal!" she said. "Poor! Poor!" responded Stevie. "Cabman poor too. He told me himself. Shame[11]!"

That little word contained all his horror at the injustice[12] of the poor cabbie having to hit the poor horse to feed his poor kids at home. And Stevie knew what it was like to be hit.

Injustice

- Do you agree with Stevie?
- Do you also agree with Winnie? Discuss in class.

9 twitch [twɪtʃ] (v.) 抽搐
10 console [kənˋsol] (v.) 安慰
11 shame [ʃem] (n.) 遺憾
12 injustice [ɪnˋdʒʌstɪs] (n.) 不公正

9. The Outrage

Mr. Verloc was depressed. He had to go to Europe, and he was depressed before the trip. When he came back ten days later he was still depressed.

Mrs. Verloc told her husband that Stevie moped[1] a lot.

"It's because of mother leaving us," she said.

Mr. Verloc didn't really listen, but when he said he was going out, his wife asked him to take Stevie with him.

"He'll lose sight[2] of me perhaps, and get lost in the street," said Mr. Verloc.

"I'll make sure that he doesn't," said his wife.

"Well, let him come along, then."

Over the next few days Mr. Verloc didn't mind taking Stevie with him. When he was ready to go out for his walk, he called the boy, in the spirit[3] in which a man calls his dog, though, of course, in a different way. One day he told his wife that he was thinking of sending Stevie out of town for a while.

"Michaelis is living in a little cottage in the country and he doesn't mind giving Stevie a room to sleep in," he said. "There are no visitors and no talk there. It will be good for Stevie."

Winnie agreed, so the next day Mr. Verloc took Stevie to the country and left him with Michaelis.

(33) Mr. Verloc went out very early the morning of the attempted bomb outrage in Greenwich Park, and Winnie was alone all day. She didn't see the newspaper. She was sitting behind the counter in the shop when he came back at dusk.

"What a horrible day," she said. "Did you go to see Stevie?"

"No! I didn't," said Mr. Verloc, and went inside the house.

She followed him after a while, to get his dinner ready. Mr. Verloc was sitting on the sofa. His teeth were rattling[4] uncontrollably and he was shaking.

This worried Winnie, but she started to lay the table for the evening meal.

"Where have you been today?" she asked.

"Nowhere," answered Mr. Verloc. "I've been to the bank."

"What for?"

"Take the money out."

"All of it? What did you do that for?"

"May need it soon."

"I don't know what you mean," said his wife.

"You know you can trust me," Mr. Verloc said.

"Oh yes. I can trust you," she said. She laid two plates, got the bread, the butter, some beef and a carving knife[5] and fork. Then she called her husband to the table, and he sat in front of her.

---

1 mope [mop] (v.) 鬱悶
2 lose sight of 看不見
3 spirit ['spɪrɪt] (n.) 念頭；心意
4 rattle ['rætl] (v.) 發出咯咯聲
5 carving knife 切肉刀

His eyes were red, his face red and his hair all messed up[1]. Winnie thought he was ill. He drank three cups of tea but didn't touch the food. Instead, he started talking about emigrating[2] to Spain or California. It was obvious to Winnie that Mr. Verloc was not in his usual state, neither physically nor mentally.

"You have a cold," she said.

At that moment the shop bell sounded. Mr. Verloc reluctantly[3] went to see the customer. They were in the shop for a long time.

When Mr. Verloc came back, he was very pale.

"What's the matter?" asked Winnie.

She could see that the customer was still in the shop. She didn't recognize him because the Assistant Commissioner was neither a regular customer nor a friend.

"I have to go out," said Mr. Verloc.

"What about the money you took out?" she asked. "Is it in your pocket? I think it's safer to . . ."

"Money! Yes, of course. Here it is." He gave Winnie the money and then he left with the stranger.

She hid the money in a pocket just as the bell rang again. A man came in, and Mrs. Verloc remembered seeing him before.

"Is your husband at home, Mrs. Verloc?" he asked.

Chief Inspector Heat was there to pay a little private visit to Mr. Verloc, hoping to get him to say something to incriminate[4] Michaelis.

---

1 mess up 混亂
2 emigrate ['ɛmə,ɡret] (v.) 移居
3 reluctantly [rɪ'lʌktəntlɪ] (adv.) 不情願地
4 incriminate [ɪn'krɪmə,net] (v.) 暗示……有罪

65

"He's just left with a stranger," Winnie told him, and from the description the Chief Inspector recognized the Assistant Commissioner. "I knew it!" he thought. He told her who he was and asked her to tell him what was going on.

He was surprised to find out that Winnie didn't know about the bomb in Greenwich.

"We've found what we believe is . . . a stolen overcoat," he said. "It's got a label sewed on the inside with your address written in ink."

"That's my brother's, then."

"Where's your brother? Can I see him?"

"No. He's been away living with a friend in the country."

"And what's the name of the friend?"

"Michaelis," said Mrs. Verloc.

"Ah! And what's your brother like? Fat and dark?"

"Oh no, that must be the thief. Stevie's slight and fair. I sewed the address inside the coat in case he got lost, as he often does."

"That means the remains I examined this morning are Mrs. Verloc's brother!" the Chief Inspector suddenly realized. "But then 'the other man' is Verloc!"

Realize

- What does Inspector Heat realize?

At that moment Mr. Verloc came back.

"What are you doing here?" he said when he saw Chief Inspector Heat.

"I came to speak with you," was the answer.

They went into the back room as Mrs. Verloc sat still, lost in confusion. But they forgot to close the door, so first she heard Chief Inspector Heat say, "You are the other man, Verloc. People told us they saw two men entering the park." And then, "We believe he stumbled against the root of a tree. Blown to small bits: body parts, gravel[1], clothing, bones—all mixed up together. I tell you they had to use a shovel to get all the pieces."

"Listen," said Verloc. "The boy was half-witted[2], irresponsible[3]. He was never going to go to prison anyway. The asylum[4] was the worst that could happen to him."

Winnie

- What does Winnie hear?
- Who is the man who "stumbled"?
- What happened to him?
- What does Verloc say about this man?
- How do you think Winnie feels?

1 gravel [ˈgrævl̩] (n.) 砂礫
2 half-witted [ˈhɑfwɪtɪd] (a.) 弱智
3 irresponsible [ˌɪrɪˈspɑnsəbl̩] (a.) 不須承擔責任的
4 asylum [əˈsaɪləm] (n.) 〔舊〕精神療養院

Chief Inspector Heat realized that Mr. Verloc's full confession[1] could do a lot of damage. It could reveal[2] the Professor's activities and create all sorts of problems while not incriminating Michaelis. He didn't want that to happen.

"My advice to you is to disappear while you can," said the Chief Inspector.

"I wish you could take me away tonight," said Mr. Verloc, looking at the shop where his wife was.

"I can imagine," said the Chief Inspector, "but I can't." He opened the door to the shop and left.

Mrs. Verloc, still behind the counter with her face in her hands, didn't look at him. She took her wedding ring and dropped it in the dustbin[3].

Dustbin

- What does Winnie put in the dustbin?
- Why?
- What do you think she will do next?

---

1 confession [kənˈfɛʃən] (n.) 坦白；供認
2 reveal [rɪˈvil] (v.) 顯露出；揭露
3 dustbin [ˈdʌstˌbɪn] (n.) 垃圾箱

10. Sir Ethelred

38

The Assistant Commissioner went straight from Brett Street to Westminster to report to the Home Secretary, Sir Ethelred, about his findings. He was received immediately.

He explained that Verloc, smothered by guilt, wanted to confess.

"What have you found out?" asked Sir Ethelred.

"The man with the bomb was Verloc's brother-in-law, a weak-minded[1] young man—his death was an accident. Michaelis had nothing to do with the whole case. What is really interesting is why Verloc organized the attack."

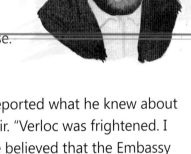

The Assistant Commissioner reported what he knew about Verloc's meeting with Mr. Vladimir. "Verloc was frightened. I imagine that he lost his head. He believed that the Embassy people are capable of publicly revealing that he's a secret agent. I don't think he's a hardened[2] criminal."

"What have you done with him?"

---

1 weak-minded ['wɪk`maɪdɪd] (a.) 怯懦的
2 hardened ['hɑrdnd] (a.) 根深蒂固的

39

"He seemed very anxious to get back to his wife in the shop and I let him go, Sir Ethelred. He will not disappear because he has got to think of the danger from his comrades[1] too. At the moment nobody knows he's involved[2], but if he tries to escape . . ."

"Very good. Is there anything more you wish to tell me now?"

"I think not, Sir Ethelred, unless I go into details . . ."

"No. No details, please. I'll talk to the Attorney General about this affair tonight. Come and see me tomorrow morning. You may go now."

---

1 comrade [ˋkɑmræd] (n.) 夥伴；同志
2 involved [ɪnˋvɑlvd] (a.) 牽扯在內的

11. Mr. and Mrs. Verloc

(40) In the house in Brett Street, Mr. Verloc didn't know what to do or how to face his wife. In his plans for the attack, nobody was going to be hurt, and definitely not Stevie. Stevie dead was a much worse problem for him than when he was alive. And the last thing he expected was that his wife would sew the boy's address inside his overcoat.

He ate the meat that was still on the table. "I didn't mean for him to get hurt," he said.

Winnie was refusing to talk to him. He tried everything: he accused Chief Inspector Heat of upsetting her; he asked her to start thinking about the future; he told her that he needed all her help to manage the shop while he was in prison. He said the arrival of the police was her fault, because of the address inside the coat, but that he forgave her.

Blame

- Who does Verloc blame for everything?
- What do you think of Verloc?
- Do you know someone who always blames someone else for everything? Tell a friend.

Then he blamed Mr. Vladimir: "You can't imagine all the stress I've been under since the meeting at the Embassy; I've been very worried and I thought many times of leaving the country, but I stayed for you."

Winnie wasn't listening. She saw herself putting Stevie to bed by the light of a single candle on the empty top floor of the lodging house. She remembered brushing his hair and helping him to get dressed; the consolations given to a small and frightened child by another child nearly as small but not quite so frightened. She saw the blows[1] intercepted[2] (often with her own head) and a door held desperately[3] shut (not for very long) against a man's rage[4]. And she heard the angry words of her violent father.

She remembered the young man she was in love with. He wanted to marry her, but he was poor and could only take her with him—there was no room for Stevie. So she married Mr. Verloc instead. To make sure that Stevie was safe.

Mr. Verloc kept talking about his worries. "Winnie, be reasonable," he said. "Look at me."

Remembering

- Who is Winnie thinking about?
- Why did she marry Mr. Verloc?

---

1 blow [blo] (n.) 揍擊
2 intercept [ˌɪntəˈsɛpt] (v.) 攔截
3 desperately [ˈdɛspərɪtlɪ] (adv.) 絕望地
4 rage [redʒ] (n.) (一陣) 狂怒

"I don't want to look at you again for as long as I live," was all she said.

Then she got up, went upstairs, and when she came back down she was dressed for going out.

"It's twenty-five past eight, Winnie. Your place this evening is here. Take your hat off. I can't let you go out," he said, and sat comfortably on the sofa. "I really wish," he said, "I could forget Greenwich Park."

The name reminded Winnie of the details of Chief Inspector Heat's story and the images flashed[1] before her eyes. Greenwich Park—smashed branches, gravel, bits of flesh and bone. They had to use a shovel to get all the pieces. She started shaking, standing near the sofa.

"Winnie, come here," he said.

She moved towards the sofa. Her hand passed over the table and she lifted the carving knife. Mr. Verloc saw the hand and the knife, but before he could do anything the knife was already planted[2] deep in his chest.

1 flash [flæʃ] (v.) 閃過
2 plant [plænt] (v.) （使勁）插入
3 gallows [ˋgæloz] (n.) 絞刑架；絞臺
4 execution [͵ɛksıˋkjuʃən] (n.) 死刑
5 authorities [əˋθɔrətız] (n.) 當局
6 carry out 執行
7 drop [drɑp] (n.) 落下
8 foot [fʊt] (n.) 〔長度單位〕呎；英尺（1 英尺 = 30.48 公分）
9 strangulation [͵stræŋgjəˋleʃən] (n.) 勒殺
10 despair [dıˋspɛr] (n.) 絕望

12. Ossipon

(43) It took Winnie Verloc some time to become aware of the result of her action, but when she finally saw all the blood, she realized it meant only one thing for her: the gallows[3]. She remembered newspaper reports about executions[4] carried out[5] in prisons. They were always "in the presence of the authorities[6]," and they ended with "the drop[7] given was fourteen feet[8]."

She became physically sick imagining the strangulation[9] and the drop cutting her head off her shoulders. No! That must never be. So she decided to throw herself into the river from one of the bridges before the police found her.

She pulled down the veil of her hat and left the house. The street frightened her, since it led either to the gallows or to the river. She felt weak, and walking was difficult. She had to hold on to a lamp-post to stop herself from falling.

"I'll never get there before morning," she thought with despair[10]. "The river is too far."

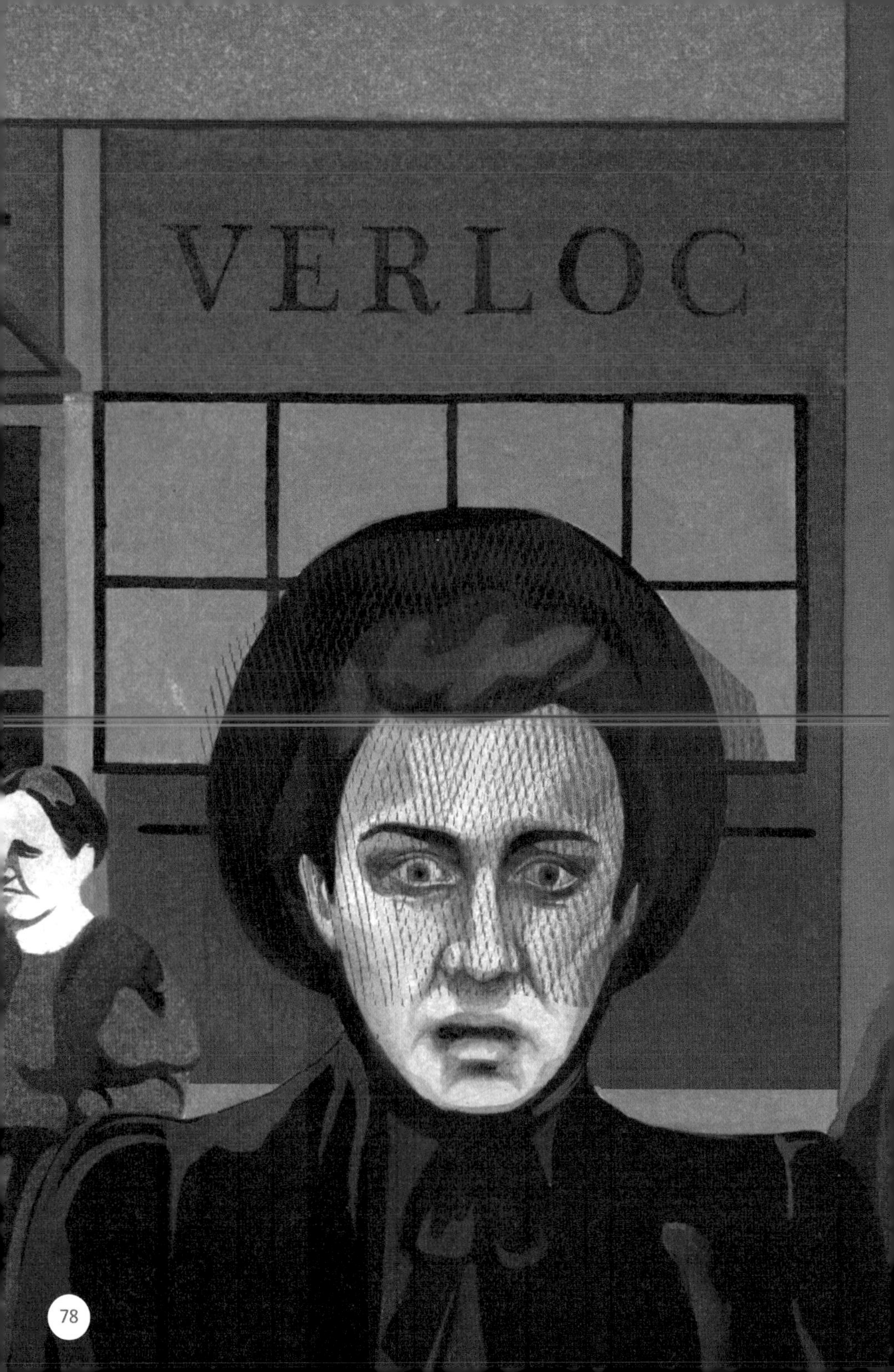
VERLOC

44 She held on, breathing heavily under the black veil. The drop given was fourteen feet.

She suddenly thought of escaping abroad. Murderers escaped abroad. Spain or California. But these were just names for her. She didn't know how to get anywhere. Murderers had friends, relations, helpers—they had knowledge. She had nothing. She was completely alone.

She started walking again, stumbling. When she looked up she saw a man's face looking closely at her veil. Ossipon, not recognizing her, thought she was just a drunk woman.

"Mr. Ossipon!" she said.

"Mrs. Verloc!" he replied.

Ossipon was there after a day of thinking: the Professor made a bomb; he gave it to Verloc; the bomb exploded in Greenwich Park killing the man who was carrying it; so Verloc was dead. Ossipon spent the day trying to decide to go and see Verloc's widow. There was money somewhere—but he was afraid that the house was watched by the police. It seemed impossible to him that someone like Mrs. Verloc could be out after dark, alone and drunk. But he decided not to question his luck.

"I recognized you from afar[1]," lied Ossipon. "I was afraid you were going to fall."

"Were you coming to the shop?" She suddenly had some hope. Maybe she wasn't alone after all.

---

1 afar [əˋfɑr] (adv.) 從遠方

"Yes. The minute I read the evening paper," explained Ossipon with great feeling, "I decided to come to you. I want to help you. I've loved you ever since I first saw you."

Ossipon calculated that no woman was capable of completely disbelieving such a statement. But he didn't know that Mrs. Verloc's response was coming from her instinct[1] of self-preservation[2]. To her, the lying Ossipon was giving her a shining message of life.

"I thought so," she said.

"I could never hide a love like this from a woman like you," he went on, while he was thinking about the business value of the shop and the amount of money that was probably in Mr. Verloc's bank account. "But you were always so distant, and I thought you loved him . . ."

"Love him!" Mrs. Verloc said, with aggressive[3] anger. "Love him! I was a young girl. I was tired. I had two people depending on me, my mother and the boy. What else could I do? I married him and I was a good wife to him for seven years. And do you know what he was? He was a devil!"

"I didn't know," said Ossipon, wondering what she was talking about, and trying to find the words. "I understand. But he's dead now."

"You guessed he was dead," she said, "so you guessed what I had to do."

---

1 instinct [ˈɪnstɪŋkt] (n.) 本能
2 self-preservation 自我保護
3 aggressive [əˈgrɛsɪv] (a.) 侵略的
4 suicide [ˈsuəˌsaɪd] (n.) 自殺
5 collapse [kəˈlæps] (v.) 崩潰

46 Ossipon started to think. He knew the dead bomber was Verloc. But how did Mrs. Verloc know? The police couldn't identify the remains, so it wasn't in the newspapers. Was she involved in the attack? Why was she so angry with her dead husband? Was it possible that her husband's death was a suicide[4], and that of the two of them, it wasn't Verloc who was the devil?

Who Was the Devil?

- What piece of information is Ossipon missing? Tell a friend.

"How did you first hear of it?" he asked.

"From the police. A chief inspector came, Chief Inspector Heat. He said they used a shovel to get all the pieces!"

"The police have already been? And what did Chief Inspector Heat do?"

"Nothing. He left. The police are on that man's side. Another one came too, maybe he was from the Embassy."

Ossipon nearly collapsed[5] under this new shock.

"Embassy! What Embassy?"

"That place in Chesham Square. I don't care. Don't ask me," she said.

(47) She then told him that she had to escape to Europe and she asked him to go with her. This whole thing was getting too complicated for Ossipon, but he kept thinking about Verloc's money. He told Winnie there were no trains until the morning, and that he could find her a room in a lodging house, but he had no money for that or for the train.

"I have enough money."

"How much have you got?"

"I have all the money that was in the bank. He gave it to me. Save me! Hide me. Don't let them have me. You must kill me first."

Ossipon was increasingly confused.

Mrs. Verloc

- Why does she need to make friends with Ossipon?
- Why was he giving her a "shining message of life"? See page 79.

"What are you afraid of?" Then he suddenly remembered: the Southampton-St Malo ship left at midnight, and there was a London-Southampton train at 10:30. They could be in France in the morning.

"Plenty of time," he said. "We're all right after all."

But Mrs. Verloc started walking towards Brett Street again.

48 "I forgot to shut the shop door as I went out," she said.

He couldn't understand why she cared—they were leaving England after all . . . But he followed her there.

The shop door was ajar[1], and the light in the back room was still on.

"I forgot the light!" Mrs. Verloc said. "Please go in and put it out, or I'll go mad."

"Where's all that money?" he said.

"I have it! Quick! Go in and put the light out."

The Light

- Why does Mrs. Verloc want Ossipon to turn out the light?
- Do you prefer telling or showing people things? Why? Tell a friend.

And so Ossipon went in, and saw Mr. Verloc resting quietly on the sofa.

He smothered[2] a scream. What was this—madness[3], a nightmare, or a trap? Was the couple planning to murder[4] him? Why? And why was Mr. Verloc pretending[5] to be asleep? Then he saw the blood, then the knife in Mr. Verloc's chest. He turned away and retched[6] violently.

---

1 ajar [ə`dʒɑr] (adv.) 半開著；微開
2 smother [`smʌðɚ] (v.) 抑制
3 madness [`mædnɪs] (n.) 經神錯亂
4 muder [`mɝdɚ] (v.) 謀殺
5 pretend [prɪ`tɛnd] (v.) 假裝；佯稱
6 retch [rɛtʃ] (v.) 作嘔；乾嘔

Mrs. Verloc came into the shop. "I will not be hanged[1]."

Ossipon put the light out. He began to think that maybe there was somebody else in the house, so he went into the shop and locked the door to the back room.

"Did you do this by yourself?" he asked.

"Yes."

"Nobody could believe it possible," he said.

He was incapable by now of judging what could be true, possible, or even probable in this extraordinary affair. He was terrified of this savage[2] woman. What did she want from him? Did she want to tell the police that he was involved in the crime? Nothing made sense.

"Was he asleep?"

"No," she said. "He was lying on the sofa comfortably—after killing the boy—my boy. I wanted to leave and never see him again. And he says to me, 'Come here,' after killing my boy."

Ossipon suddenly understood: the dead man in Greenwich Park was that half-witted young man.

Now he was even more terrified of her—the sister of the degenerate, a degenerate herself of a murdering type. He was trapped. Nobody was going to believe that she was her husband's killer, and as long as they stayed at the house she was going to be able to claim that he was the killer.

Suddenly he made a decision.

"Let's get out, or we'll miss the train."

---

1 hang [hæŋ] (v.) 吊死 (三態：hang, hanged, hanged)
2 savage ['sævɪdʒ] (a.) 殘暴的
3 gratitude ['grætə,tjud] (n.) 感激之情；感恩

(50)   They took a cab to the station, and Ossipon explained his plan.

"When we arrive, you must go into the station ahead of me, as if we do not know each other. The police may be there. Alone you are only a woman taking a train. But I am known. With me, they may guess you are Mrs. Verloc running away. I will get the tickets, and put yours in your hand as I pass you. Then you will go into the first-class ladies' waiting room, and sit there until ten minutes before the train leaves. Then you will come out and go to the platform first. I will follow you. By the way, I need to have the money for the tickets now."

She gave him a little bag with all the money.

"Do you know how much money there is in it?" he asked.

"No. I didn't count it."

They arrived at the station. Ossipon remained behind and the plan was carried out. They boarded the train separately, and they met inside.

"Go and sit at the other end of the carriage, my dear—it's safer," said Ossipon.

She looked at him with gratitude³. "I will live all my days for you!"

At last the train began to move. Ossipon crossed the carriage in two long steps, opened the door, and jumped out of the train.

While the train left the station, he walked home, with his pockets full of money, and went to sleep.

The next day he bought the newspaper. There was an article in it that ended with the words: "Nobody will ever be able to solve the mystery of this act of madness or despair." The headline read: "Suicide of Lady Passenger on Boat to France."

He became unable to throw the newspaper away. The rest of the world was never going to be able to solve the mystery. But he started drinking heavily every day, trying to forget the truth that stayed with him for the rest of his life.

AFTER READING

1 Talk about the story

1 Answer the questions.

a Did you enjoy reading the story? Why?/Why not?

b In your opinion, which is the most interesting character? Why?

c Which two characters did you like the least?

d Do you think there is a hero in this story? If you do, who is it, and why?

e Did any part of the story surprise you? Why?

f What do you think happened to Ossipon, the Professor and Winnie's mother after the end of the story?

g Do you think the story is realistic?

h Would you like to see a film version of this story?

2 Share your ideas with the class.

3 Work in small groups. Make a list of films or stories you know in which:

a everything goes wrong.

b someone pays for someone else's mistakes.

c someone thinks he or she is a lot more intelligent than they are.

4 Compare your group's lists with the other groups'. Did anybody include the same films?

1 Read the sentences and tick (√) the correct answer.

		True	False	Doesn't say
a	Verloc is paid a lot of money by the Embassy.	☐	☐	☐
b	Verloc is an anarchist.	☐	☐	☐
c	Mr. Vladimir wants an outrage because he wants repression in the UK.	☐	☐	☐
d	Verloc agrees with Mr. Vladimir's ideas about what to do.	☐	☐	☐
e	The Professor is a member of Verloc's anarchist group.	☐	☐	☐
f	Verloc explains his plan to the Professor in detail.	☐	☐	☐
g	The bomb was in the tin can.	☐	☐	☐
h	Stevie knew there was a bomb in the tin can.	☐	☐	☐
i	Michaelis knew about Verloc's plan to bomb the Observatory.	☐	☐	☐
j	Both Chief Inspector Heat and the Assistant Commissioner solve the case.	☐	☐	☐

2 Complete the sentences with the words from the box.

Ossipon	a telegram	Chief Inspector Heat
Verloc	the newspapers (x2)	the Assistant Commissioner
Winnie (x2)		

a) Ossipon found out about the bomb from _____.

b) The Professor found out about the bomb from

_____.

c) Chief Inspector Heat found out about the bomb from

_____.

d) Verloc found out what happened from _____.

e) The Assistant Commissioner discovered what happened from

_____.

f) Chief Inspector Heat discovered what happened from

_____.

g) Winnie discovered what happened from _____.

h) The Home Secretary found out what happened from

_____.

i) Ossipon found out what happened from _____.

3 Read the dictionary definition of "at cross purposes" and answer the questions.

> **at cross purposes** *adverb* when two or more people do not understand each other because they are talking about different things but they don't know that

a) Which two characters talk at cross purposes in the story?

b) In what way are they at cross purposes?

c) Which two characters are not at cross purposes, but one of them doesn't understand the other because the other is hiding his real reasons?

d) What is the real reason the other character is hiding?

e) What is the result?

4 Discuss your ideas in a small group or with a friend.

1 Read the sentences and tick (√) T (True) or F (False).

T F (a) Verloc married Winnie for love.

T F (b) Winnie married Verloc for love.

T F (c) The only person who Winnie loves is Stevie.

T F (d) Stevie cares about everybody, including strangers.

T F (e) Verloc's actions are the result of his high ideals of social justice.

T F (f) Ossipon's actions are the result of his high ideals of social justice.

T F (g) Chief Inspector Heat wants to incriminate Michaelis because he really thinks he's involved.

T F (h) The Assistant Commissioner doesn't want to incriminate Michaelis for personal reasons.

2 Answer the questions. You can write more than one character, and you can use the same character many times.

Mr. Verloc	Winnie	Ossipon
Mr. Vladimir	Stevie	the Professor

(a) Thinks he/she is cleverer than he/she is: _____

(b) Thinks he/she is cleverer than everybody else: _____

(c) Is unable to imagine what it must be like to be in someone else's situation. _____

(d) Is able to imagine what it must be like to be in someone else's situation. _____

(e) Feels other people's pain all the time: _____

(f) Pretends to be something he/she is not: _____

(g) Is always thinking about the advantages he/she can get in every situation: _____

(h) Gave up something important for the benefit of someone else:

3 Match the pictures to the descriptions of the characters.

_____ ① He thinks that Mr. Verloc is an idiot and is rude to him.

_____ ② He's trying to do his job, but at first he has the wrong idea.

_____ ③ He finds out the truth, but for the wrong reasons.

_____ ④ He is very powerful and very busy.

_____ ⑤ He feels everybody's pain.

_____ ⑥ He is angry, full of hatred, and not good at anything in particular.

_____ ⑦ He builds and sells bombs.

_____ ⑧ He works at night, he's very poor and has three children.

4 Read this text and answer the question.

> Stevie knew very well that hot iron applied to one's skin hurts very much.

What does this sentence tell us about Stevie's past?

1 Complete the mind-map with the words in the box.

incriminate
confess
confession
investigate
commit a crime
execution
feel guilt
find evidence
sentence
be a suspect
trial
go to prison
arrest (n.)
arrest (v.)
be out on parole

what the
criminal does

----

what the
police does

CRIME

events

----

2 Do you know other
words you can add
to this mind map?

3 Complete the sentences with words from Exercise 1.

a) Chief Inspector Heat started to _____ the explosion at the hospital.

b) Michaelis was out of prison _____.

c) The Assistant Commissioner didn't _____ Verloc after he confessed.

d) Winnie decided to kill herself to avoid _____.

e) Verloc confessed because of the _____ he was feeling.

f) Chief Inspector Heat was hoping to _____ Michaelis.

g) The Assistant Commissioner didn't want Michaelis to be a _____.

4 Match the words and the definitions.

_____ 1 repression
_____ 2 target
_____ 3 blow
_____ 4 an outrage
_____ 5 legality
_____ 6 middle class

a) What you receive if someone or something hits you with force.

b) The use of force or violence to stop political activities and expression.

c) The social class of people who are paid a good salary for their work.

d) What you aim at.

e) A shocking act of violence.

f) The things that are required and allowed by law.

5 Complete this paragraph with words from Exercise 4.

Mr. Vladimir wants Mr. Verloc to commit (a) _____ in London. He thinks that the British authorities are too worried about (b) _____ and that something is needed to cause (c) _____ from the police. He wants the (d) _____ to be afraid, and he thinks that royalty and religion should not be the (e) _____. He thinks that an attack on astronomy is the (f) _____ that is needed to shock the British.

1 Complete these first conditionals with the correct form of the verbs in brackets.

a) If we _____ (arrest) him, the police _____ (take) him back to prison.

b) If he _____ (go) back to prison, he _____ (die) smothered in his fat, and she _____ (never/forgive) me.

c) A bomb like that _____ (explode) if you _____ (give) it a sharp shock.

d) He _____ (be) in danger from his colleagues if he _____ (try) to escape.

e) If a spy from the police _____ (ask) you for your wares, they _____ (arrest) you with the proof in their hands.

f) They _____ (kill) me on the gallows if they _____ (find) me.

2 Re-write these sentences in the passive form.

a) Cats and dogs easily distracted him.

b) When he arrived, somebody took him into a small room.

c) Someone switched on the detonator.

d) What Chief Inspector Heat saw shocked him.

e) After they released Michaelis from prison, a rich old lady decided to help him.

f) They accidentally killed a policeman.

g) The Home Secretary received the Assistant Commissioner immediately.

h) Before Mr. Verloc could do anything Winnie planted the knife in his chest.

3 Re-write these sentences using the correct form of the words in brackets.

a It's better for us if they forget their own principles of legality.(we/want)
b Please make my apologies. (ask/his wife)
c Why don't you take Stevie with you? (ask/her husband)
d Please, Mr. Ossipon, leave with me. (Winnie/want)

4 Re-write the sentences in the past simple, using the correct form of have to.

a There are pieces of him everywhere. We need use a shovel.
b He whips the horse because he needs to earn his money.
c Mr. Verloc must go to Europe.
d She needs to hold on to a lamp-post to stop herself from falling.

5 Read the definitions. Can you find an example of figurative language on page 33?

> figurative language the use of words to mean something different from their basic meaning. For example, "you're an angel" does not mean "you're a supernatural being" but "you're very good/generous".

> literal meaning exactly the basic meaning of words. For example, "you're a supernatural being" is the literal meaning of "you're an angel".

6 Read these texts from the story and answer the questions.

> **1**
>
> "Teeth and ears mark the criminal? And what about the law that marks him even better? The law is a red-hot branding instrument invented by those who have too much food to protect themselves against the hungry. Can't you smell and hear the skin of the people burn? That's how criminals are made."

> **2**
>
> "Do you know how I call the nature of the present economic conditions?I call it cannibalistic. That's what it is! They are feeding their greed on the flesh and the warm blood of the people."

a) Who says these things?

b) What does he mean in 1?

c) What does Stevie understand?

d) What does he mean in 2?

e) What does Stevie understand?

f) Can Stevie understand figurative language? Why?/Why not?

g) Can you think of figurative language you use every day in your own language?

6 Plot and theme

1 Number the events in the order they happened.
Write the numbers in the first box before the sentences.

☐ ☐ [a] Stevie stumbles and dies in the explosion.

☐ ☐ [b] There's an explosion in Greenwich Park and Chief Inspector Heat starts to investigate.

☐ ☐ [c] Winnie kills herself.

☐ ☐ [d] Winnie hears the conversation between Chief Inspector Heat and Mr. Verloc and understands what happened.

☐ ☐ [e] Winnie doesn't want to be hanged in the gallows, so she decides to kill herself by jumping in the river.

☐ ☐ [f] Mr. Vladimir tells Mr. Verloc to commit an outrage.

☐ ☐ [g] Winnie's mother moves to the almshouse and Stevie feels sorry for the horse and the cabbie.

☐ ☐ [h] Mr. Verloc takes Stevie to Greenwich Park and gives him a bomb to place in the Observatory.

☐ ☐ [i] Ossipon pretends to leave with Winnie, but at the last minute jumps from the train.

☐ ☐ [j] When Mr. Verloc tries to stop her from leaving, Winnie kills him.

2 Now number the events in the order in which they are told in the story. Write the numbers in the second box before the sentences.

3 Look at the two numbers for each event and answer the questions.

[a] Are they the same for each event?

[b] Did the author tell the story in chronological order?

[c] What did the author do?

4 Read these texts from the story and answer the questions.

> **1**
>
> "We want something that will cause repression. England is silly with its respect for individual freedom. I have an idea. We want the middle class to feel fear, and we need a series of outrages to do that."

> **2**
>
> "We want them to forget their own rules and principles of legality. I will be very pleased when the police start shooting us in the streets and the public is happy. That will be when their morality starts to disintegrate. That will be the beginning of our victory. That is what we should try to achieve."

a) Who says 1?

b) Who says 2?

c) What is their purpose? Tick (√) the correct answer.
☐ legality
☐ repression
☐ a cause

d) How do they both want to achieve it?
☐ with legality
☐ with terrorist attacks
☐ with more freedom

e) Look at your answer to question c. Why does Character 2 think it will be the beginning of their victory? What is his final purpose?

f Look at your answer to question e. Does Character 1 want the same?

g Do you think the author agrees with these two characters? Why?/Why not?

5 Read the text from the story and answer the questions.

> That little word, "shame", contained all his horror at the injustice of the poor cabbie having to hit the poor horse to feed his poor kids at home.

a Whose thoughts are these?

b Do you think the author agrees with this character? Why?/Why not?

LIFE SKILL

TERRORISM

Read the text and answer the questions.

TERRORISM *noun* [U] the use of violence for political or religious purposes

HISTORY OF THE WORD

The word "terrorism" was first used to describe the activities of the French government in 1793–1794 during the French Revolution. This period was called the Reign of Terror because the government used violence, repression and fear against its own citizens to control them. In one year there were 16,594 official death sentences. Suspects were arrested and sent to prison without trial, and many died there or killed themselves.

WHAT IS TERRORISM?

Terrorism is violent behavior designed to create fear in a community for political or religious purposes. A terrorist act can be committed by individuals, groups or states. Some individuals commit an outrage because they are angry with their government, with a company or with somebody else. They may use bombs or guns and shoot everybody they see. These are different from terrorist acts because they haven't got a political plan.

Sometimes a government encourages a terrorist group against a common enemy. After the enemy is defeated, the terrorist group often attacks the country whose government encouraged it.

Not everybody agrees about who is a terrorist and who is not, and sometimes opinions change over time. Of course, terrorists never call themselves terrorists.

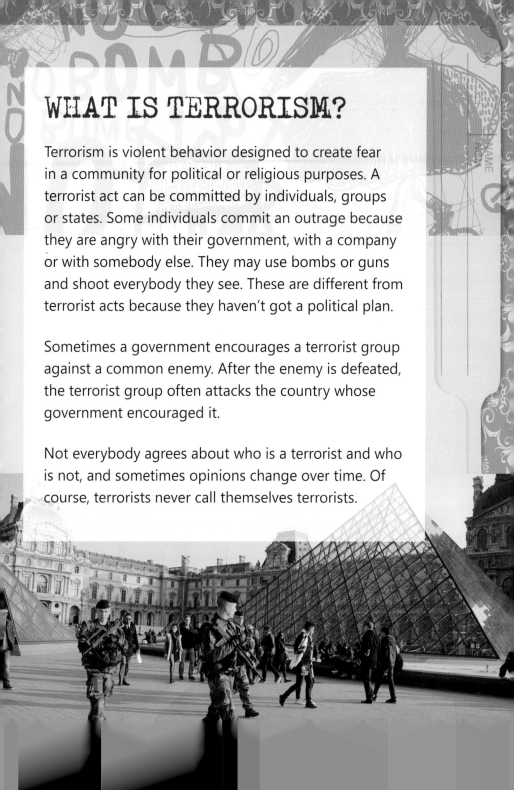

TYPES OF TERRORISM

Some terrorist groups attack only politicians and political targets. These sometimes plant[1] a bomb and then call the police so that people can be moved from the place and only the place is damaged. Their purpose is to let a government know that they can kill if they want to, to force[2] a political change.

Others attack ordinary people, especially in crowded places, and turn the attack into a spectacle[3] for television, the newspapers and social media. Their purpose is to kill as many people as possible, make people fear that all places can be a target and nobody is safe, and to get as much publicity[4] as possible.

One of the results of terrorism can be repression and less freedom for everybody. Sometimes this is the real aim.

ENDING TERRORISM

Depending on the motivation of the terrorist group, there are different ways in which terrorism ended in the past.

One is because it achieved its purpose, so there was no reason for it to continue. In other cases the violence stopped because the group was included in a political process. Some terrorist groups ended because there was no public support for their purpose, or because different sub-groups started fighting each other. Others died when their leaders were arrested or killed. Others, however, had to be defeated and destroyed by force.

1 plant [plænt] (v.) 設置
2 force [fors] (v.) 迫使
3 spectacle ['spɛktəkl̩] (n.) 公開展示
4 publicity [pʌb'lɪsətɪ] (n.) (公眾的) 注意

1 Which aspects of terrorism described in this text can you find in *The Secret Agent*?

2 Do you know of any country in recent history that is similar to France during the Reign of Terror?

3 Do you know of anybody in recent history that is similar to Mr Vladimir?

4 Do you know of any person or group in recent history that is similar to the Professor?

5 Do you know of any group that stopped using violence because they entered a political process?

6 Do you know of any group that uses violence and is not interested in entering a political process?

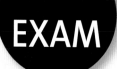

 Cambridge English: Preliminary English Test Reading Part 1

A group of students are making a film version of *The Secret Agent*. Look at the text in each question. What does it say? Tick (√) the correct letter (A, B or C).

1

> If we want to use my uncle's shop for the scene between Winnie and Heat, we'll have to do it this Saturday, before my uncle comes back from holiday. Let me know if that's OK. Jim

- ☐ (a) The scene between Winnie and Heat is going to be done in Jim's uncle's shop today.
- ☐ (b) If the scene between Winnie and Heat can't be done this Saturday, they will need to find another shop.
- ☐ (c) Jim's uncle doesn't want them to do the scene in his shop this Saturday.

2

> Old clothes gravel and a pair of unwanted shoes needed tomorrow for the hospital scene. Please be aware that the shoes will be covered in red paint. Please contact Sam.

- ☐ (a) The hospital room will be painted red tomorrow.
- ☐ (b) Sam will play the part of Stevie.
- ☐ (c) The shoes' owner should expect the shoes to be damaged.

3 Billy, come on, it's a film: your clothes don't actually have to be dirty for your scene with Ossipon. They only need to look it! Carl

☐ [a] Billy's clothes can look dirty and be clean.
☐ [b] The actor playing Ossipon complained about Billy's clothes.
☐ [c] Billy needs to look like Ossipon.

4 Sam, please ask Bob to make the horse go slower.

☐ [a] Sam and Bob are friends.
☐ [b] Bob plays the cabbie;
☐ [c] Bob needs to slow the horse down.

5 We need to have the blue coat made by Monday. Any progress? Pete

☐ [a] Pete wants to know if the blue coat will be ready on Monday.
☐ [b] They haven't got a blue coat.
☐ [c] There is no progress about the blue coat.

6 EVERYBODY: it might rain later today. Be ready to change plans.

☐ [a] Plans have changed.
☐ [b] There is a possibility that it will rain.
☐ [c] It will almost certainly rain.

TEST

52 **1** Listen and tick (√) the correct picture.

a 1 2

b 1 2

c 1 2

d 1 2

2 Choose the correct answer 1, 2, 3 or 4.

_____ a Why didn't Winnie marry the young man she loved?

1 Because her father didn't let her.

2 Because her mother wanted her to work at the lodging house.

3 Because he was too poor to take Stevie, too.

4 Because he never asked her to marry him.

_____ b Why does Stevie get upset when he sees violence?

1 Because he's a pacifist.

2 Because his father was violent towards him.

3 Because he doesn't understand.

4 Because that's what Winnie taught him.

_____ c What adjective best describes Mr. Vladimir's behavior towards Verloc?

1 rude   2 formal   3 cold   4 friendly

_____ d What do the group of anarchists want to achieve?

1 terrorism   2 better government

3 repression   4 it's not clear

_____ e Why does the Assistant Commissioner want to stop Heat from incriminating Michaelis?

1 Because he believes that Michaelis is not responsible.

2 Because the Home Secretary asks him to.

3 Because he likes Michaelis.

4 Because he's worried about the effect on his relationship with the great lady.

_____ f Why does Heat tell Verloc to leave instead of arresting him?

1 Because he feels sorry for him.

2 To save himself a lot of problems.

3 Because he feels sorry for Mrs. Verloc.

4 To annoy the Assistant Commissioner.

Secret Intelligence Service

TOP SECRET

Work in small groups. Make a poster or a video about a good spy story, real or fictional.

Find images and include the answers to these questions:

- Was the spy real or fictional?
- Was it one individual or a group?
- Which country were they from?
- Who did they work for?
- What was their purpose?
- Did they achieve it?
- How do we know their story?
- What happened to them?
- Are there books, films or websites about them?
- Are there any similarities between them and *The Secret Agent*?
- What do you think of them?

作者簡介

P. 4

1857 年，約瑟夫·康拉德（Joseph Conrad）生於別爾基切夫（位於烏克蘭）。當時的別爾基切夫市屬於俄羅斯帝國的版圖，但曾隸屬波蘭的領土範圍。他出身波蘭家庭，家族裡不乏知識分子與政運人士，為恢復波蘭的政權統一和獨立建國而奮鬥。因此，雖然身分上是俄羅斯人，但他以波蘭人自居。

他的學業表現不算優異，卻飽讀詩書與莎士比亞文學，而且説得一口流利法文。很小的時候，就展現出説故事的才華。他 16 歲時先加入法國商船，再轉至英國商船。他有十九餘年的跑船經驗，環遊世界之際還晉升至船長職位。

他畢生深受健康欠佳與憂鬱症之苦，二十歲時甚至自殺未遂。 1886 年，他取得英國公民身分。 1894 年，他離開商船，投入寫作。兩年後與英國人潔西·喬治（Jessie George）結縭，膝下育有二子。

雖然英語是康拉德的第三語言，甚至是從二十歲才開始學習英語，但他儼然成為享譽盛名且具影響力的英國作家。他筆下的故事主要描述人們面對極端情境時的反應，並以當年跑船的經驗為寫作靈感。

1924 年，他於肯特郡的宅邸辭世，可能是死於心臟病發。

本書簡介

P. 6

《祕密間諜》的故事背景設於倫敦，主人翁是一名擁有雙重身分的維拉克先生，他表面上是販售廢棄舊物的商店老闆，私底下卻是他國政府的間諜。他和年輕太太溫妮、岳母，以及具有學習障礙的 20 歲出頭小舅子史提夫，一起住在店面樓上的公寓。故事情節亦包含一個無政府主義團體、至少一名恐怖分子、兩名警官和若干政府官員。

本故事靈感來自真實事件：1894 年，名為馬歇爾·伯丁（Martial Bourdin）的法國無政府主義者，於格林威治皇家天文台附近的格林威治公園，以炸彈客之姿自爆。此事件一直是未解之謎：無從得知攻擊動機、目標或爆炸當下的實情。雖然康拉德能收集的訊息有限，卻有辦法以這場無法解釋的慘烈死亡攻擊事件做為小說主軸。

《祕密間諜》雖於 1907 年出版，故事主題卻十分現代，恐怖主義、間諜行動和權力鬥爭仍是現今常見的新聞頭條。康拉德向讀者揭露恐怖主義背後的思維，以及恐怖分子與掌權人士透過恐怖主義的手段，想達到何種目的。《祕密間諜》可說是一部充滿間諜、偵探和心理劇的小說。

真實檔案 「間諜」奧立佛與「佩特里奇革命」

P. 8

英國雖然於 1215 年建立議會民主制度，但到了 1817 年，具有投票權的人民仍低於 3%。1775 年，北美十三殖民地發起對抗英國的「獨立戰爭」，希冀創建第一個真正的民主國家。1789 年爆發的「法國大革命」，推翻君主專制政體而建立共和國。英國勞工從報上得知此消息後，非常吃味。

而作物歉收頻傳與進口穀物課徵新稅等規定，導致糧食物價高漲，讓情況雪上加霜。

政府意識到，逐漸成形的政治團體會紛紛要求修法，來讓勞工擁有投票權。因此設立了能夠滲透此類團體的間諜與情報人員網絡，來向政府回報情資。政府要找理由來遏制此類團體，因此間諜與情報人員一定得找出個理由才行。

> 1817 年的投票條件包含以下三項：
> 必須是男性
> 必須超過 21 歲
> 必須擁有有價資產

間諜奧立佛

　　威廉二世・奧立佛（William J. Oliver），人稱「間諜奧立佛」，他負責滲透英格蘭北部德比郡的勞工團體。他向政府回報情資，並針對政府的需求製造理由。他告訴勞團中的人，包括曼徹斯特等大城市的人們十分憤怒，武裝的勞工已準備前往倫敦示威，欲逼迫政府釋出勞工投票權。

　　1817 年 6 月 9 日，三百名男子離開佩特里奇村莊（Pentrich），與諾丁漢（Nottingham）北部相距 14 英里。他們往南，向倫敦移動，抵達伊斯伍德村莊（Eastwood）後，才發現步入重兵圍剿的陷阱。他們試圖逃離，但有 46 人以叛國罪之名遭到逮捕。

　　政府為了殺雞儆猴，因此重罰判刑：有三人遭判死刑，23 人被流放至澳洲坐牢。沒有人回到祖國，而他們的眷屬亦被迫遠離家園。間諜奧立佛爾後來前往南非效命。

　　1918 年，經過多次小型改革，所有 21 歲以上的男性和 30 歲以上的女性，均能享有投票權。

> 閱讀《祕密間諜》時，請思考以下問題
>
> 故事內容是否與「佩特里奇革命」有任何相似之處？

深入了解

何謂「貝特魯大屠殺」（Peterloo Massacre）？
何謂「憲章運動」（Chartist Movement）？
女性於何時擁有滿 21 歲即可投票的權利？
男性與女性於何時擁有滿 18 歲即可投票的權利？

真實檔案 劍橋間諜

P. 12

　　「劍橋間諜」的成員有四名男子，他們於 1930 年代在劍橋大學相識，爾後成為第二次世界大戰與後續冷戰時期為蘇聯效力的祕密間諜。許多著作與電影以他們的故事為主軸。

安東尼·布朗特（Anthony Blunt）是四人裡最年長的一人，當時他在劍橋大學授課，並陸續招募哈洛·金·菲比（Harold "Kim" Philby）、唐諾·麥克林（Donald Maclean）以及蓋·柏格斯（Guy Burgess）。後來有一位俄羅斯間諜向英國投誠，表示劍橋間諜成員尚有第五人，但至今仍無法證實此人身分。

這個間諜四人幫長久以來均未被發現真實身分，原因其一在於他們擁有顯赫背景，英國當局壓根想不到，來自富裕家庭且擁有劍橋大學學歷的這些人會背叛祖國，成為蘇聯的祕密間諜。

四人幫離開劍橋後，於各領域擔任重要職務：安東尼·布朗特在二戰時期服務於軍情五處（MI5），爾後成為為英國女皇效力的重要藝術歷史學家，並於 1956 年受封為騎士；蓋·柏格斯成為一名記者，先後服務於英國廣播公司（BBC）和軍情六處（MI6）；唐諾·麥克林則服務於英國外交部；菲比在二戰期間任職於維也納，協助躲避德國納粹的難民，後來擔任《泰晤士報》等各大報社的記者，最後加入軍情六處（MI6）。

身為蘇聯祕密間諜的菲比，在軍情六處任職期間，成為反蘇聯單位的主管，甚至到美國擔任英國情報總長。他在軍情六處的地位意味著，蘇聯祕密情報特務組織 KGB 不僅能藉此獲得情資，還能確保其他劍橋間諜不被發現。因此，當軍情六處察覺外交部可能有內鬼時，菲比率先獲知柏格斯和麥克林已遭當局懷疑。他通知二人，並協助他們投靠蘇聯。

然而，經過此事之後，他自己也成了嫌疑犯而只好辭職，亦於不久後投誠蘇聯。這三名劍橋間諜一直居留蘇聯至終老。

1963 年，英國政府發現安東尼·布朗特的間諜身分。政府以豁免權做為安東尼交換情報的條件。雖然他透露極少情資，卻未因此入獄，並且繼續居住在倫敦。

英國祕密情報局

軍情五處是英國國內的情報單位，肩負的任務是過止英國境內可能出現的恐怖攻擊與間諜行動，並由內政部掌管。

軍情六處屬於由外交部掌管的國外情報單位。1909 年後任職的所有軍情六處處長，只會以字母 C 簽署文件，以便隱匿身分。

1. 維拉克先生

P. 23

維拉克先生出門時，都會讓小舅子史提夫看店，而維拉克夫人則負責照料史提夫。店面與樓上公寓的空間狹隘，彷彿是坐落於貝瑞特街上的一個方盒子。商店櫥窗展示的商品既廉價又蒙上一層灰，進門的顧客大都看似經濟拮据。

大門上方掛著一個門鈴，門鈴一響，維拉克先生就會從店裡後側的休息室走出來。他身材臃腫，髮色偏深，眼皮下垂，一副穿戴整齊的樣子，整天坐陣在雜亂的床鋪上。然後，他會以明顯過高的價格幫顧客結帳。

有時門鈴一響，接待的是維拉克夫人。溫妮·維拉克夫人年輕貌美，但對於店內顧客以及走進後側休息室的特殊訪客似乎興趣缺缺。而商店大門是這棟房子的唯一進出口。

溫妮的母親也跟他們一起住，她體態豐腴，雙腳腫脹，不良於行，已經喪偶。她以前有一棟短租公寓，當時溫妮協助她照料房客起居，而她與維拉克先生就是在那裡相識的。他常有前往歐洲的神祕行程，每次回國都會待在那裡。

P. 24

兩人結縭時，溫妮的母親賣掉短租公寓，因為那會防礙維拉克先生的另一個事業，但他並未說明是什麼樣的事業。他曾告訴溫妮，自己的工作牽涉到政治，而溫妮的母親也很難再知道更多。

夫妻倆帶著溫妮的母親和弟弟搬到新家。溫妮很疼愛需要呵護的弟弟，而維拉克先生親切又大方，因此溫妮的母親覺得，可憐的小兒子終於能在這個艱難世道擁有安全的避風港。

溫妮的弟弟史提夫二十三歲，體型瘦弱，一頭金髮，照顧起來不容易。他雖然讀寫不成問題，但是當個打雜小弟還是不太稱職。他常會忘記傳話內容，很容易因為街上的貓狗而分心，還會迷路。他對事情感到困惑不解時，就會結巴。不過他還是以無盡的親情之愛，幫忙姊姊處理家事，而溫妮就像母親一樣的照顧他。

在一個特別的早上，維拉克先生十點半就出門前往海德公園，將房子、家務事和店內生意拋諸身後。

維拉克先生

• 有誰住在維拉克先生的家中？
• 維拉克先生以何維生？

2. 大使館

P. 26

對維拉克先生來說，早上十點半是一個早得反常的出門時間。他觀察車水馬龍的街道，很欣慰能看到城市富足繁榮的景象。所有的人民都需要受到保護，安全是人民得以享有富裕豪奢生活的首要條件。

他是個懶散的人，或者說，他認為不管人做了什麼事，都不會產生任何的影響。他還有一種勞工所沒有的氣質，也就是利用人性的弱點、愚昧或最低度的恐懼來賺錢的那種氣質。

他和一家大使館有生意往來。他口袋裡塞著一張紙條，指示他那天早上前往大使館。他抵達後，就被帶到一個小房間，裡面擺設一張沉重的辦公桌和幾張椅子。大使館官員馮特先生，手上拿著一些報告走進來，維拉克先生認出報告上自己的筆跡。

馮特先生開口：「我這裡有一些你提交的報告。我們對於這個國家的警方所採取的態度不甚滿意，他們太溫和。我們需要製造能夠吸引警方注意力、讓法官加重判刑的事件。這樣的事件將能提高現在的緊張情勢……」

P. 27

「現在的緊張情勢已經有危險之虞。」維拉克先生打斷他說道：「我過去十二個月的報告寫得很清楚。」

馮特先生說：「我已經看過你的報告，那毫無作用呀。」

屋裡一片寂靜。這時馮特先生說話了。

「你太胖了。」他接著說：「我覺得你該見見瓦拉迪莫先生，請在這裡稍候。」隨即離開房間。

維拉克先生的額頭冒出豆大汗

珠，一動也不敢動。

　　一位僕人走進來，帶他前往一樓，幫他開門，讓他進入廳內。廳室很寬敞，有三面窗戶。看似位高權重的一名年輕人，坐在木製大辦公桌前的大型扶手椅上。他先和即將離開的馮特先生用法文交談：「親愛的，你說得沒錯，這個畜生，確實很胖。」

　　身為大使館首席祕書長的瓦拉迪莫先生，可說是上流社會的寵兒。他說道：「我想你應該聽得懂法文？」

P. 28

　　維拉克先生表示他聽得懂，然後低喃的說些他在法國從軍的事。突然間，瓦拉迪莫先生開始說出一口毫無外國口音的流利英文。

　　「你為我們的大使館效力多久了？」他問道。

　　「十一年了，從已故的史托特沃騰漢男爵時代起，我就在這兒了。」維拉克先生答道。

　　「史托特沃騰漢男爵是個耳根子軟的老人家，現在局勢已經不一樣了。你說說看，為什麼讓你自己落到這個田地？看看你的德性，你是挨餓的無產階級、孤注一擲的社會主義者，還是無政府主義者？你到底是哪一種人？」

　　「無政府主義者。」維拉克先生如是說。

　　「你真的認為有人會相信你嗎？」

瓦拉迪莫先生接著說：「連呆子都不會相信，這些人也是呆子。你呢，就是個荒謬至極、算不上聰明、還很懶散的人。從我們的文件看來，你過去三年什麼都沒做，還拿錢。」

　　「什麼都沒做？」維拉克大喊：「我有好幾次避免了……」

P. 30

　　瓦拉迪莫先生打斷他的話：「一般來說，預防勝於治療的觀念是不智之舉，而用在這個案子就更蠢。問題已經存在，我們要的不是預防，我們要的是治療。現在是我在管，我明確的告訴你，你要想辦法證明自己。沒績效，就拿不到錢。」

　　維拉克先生很意外，開始害怕起來。

　　「我們需要能夠嚇阻群眾的辦法。」瓦拉迪莫先生說：「英格蘭尊重個人自由的做法太愚昧。我有個想法。」

　　瓦拉迪莫先生說明想法的時候，透露出他其實不太了解革命圈子，也讓沉默的維拉克先生感到震驚。

　　「我們希望中產階級產生恐懼，所以需要一連串的暴行來達成目的。所謂『暴行』，不一定要十分暴力，而是能夠營造出戒慎恐懼的氛圍，然後我們應該以建物為目標。維拉克先生，現在中產階級奉為圭臬的思想潮流是什麼？」瓦拉迪莫先生說。

　　維拉克先生聳聳肩。

你一個月的時間，否則就切斷你和我們之間的關係。」

瓦拉迪莫先生

- 你對他的點子有何想法？
- 你覺得他是什麼樣的人？
- 目前在你的國家中，你想得到有什麼人物的性格和他相似嗎？

「你真是連腦子都懶得動。」瓦拉迪莫先生說：「你仔細聽好，現在的中產階級不信貴族或宗教那一套，因此我們不能將皇宮和教會當作目標。目前最新的思想潮流是科學，攻擊事件想要成功，就要展現出摧毀社會的決心。任何擁有體面工作的人，都篤信知識與科學這兩件事，所以你覺得針對天文學領域進行攻擊怎麼樣？」

P. 31

維拉克先生心裡覺得這個主意很差勁。

「文明世界的人都聽說過格林威治，格林威治皇家天文台會是最棒的攻擊目標。」瓦拉迪莫先生沾沾自喜地說道。

維拉克先生啞口無言。

「你可以走了。」瓦拉迪莫先生說道：「我們需要炸彈攻擊事件，我給

3. 會面

P. 32

過了幾天，維拉克先生的政治小組來到他位於貝瑞特街的商店，並於店內後側休息室會面。

麥可利斯開始發表言論，由於他過於肥胖，因此他的說話能力受到影響。入獄十五年後，他假釋出獄，現在帶著一肚子肥肉和一張臃腫的臉。在獄中期間，他構想出一個公平社會的願景，並且一如往常，以模稜兩可卻又充滿熱忱的措辭高談闊論。

在休息室的另一側，缺牙的卡爾·楊特咯咯的笑。他自稱「恐怖分子」，又老又禿頭，死寂的眼神裡滿是高漲恨意。

他說道：「我一直希望能有一群人，願意以人道主義為出發點而殺戮與慷慨赴義。這就是我的夢想。」

而麥可利斯仍在講話。他總是在

那只有四面牆陪伴的孤獨牢房裡，將心裡想的事説出來。他不擅長與人討論，別人的聲音會干擾他的思緒，所以他無視他人的存在而繼續發言。

休息室開始變得悶熱，維拉克先生打開通往廚房的門扉。此時可看見史提夫安靜的正襟危坐於桌邊，不停地在畫圓圈。他只會畫圓圈。

P. 33

人稱「醫師」的亞歷山大·奧斯朋是醫學院肄業生，他走到史提夫身後瞧了一眼。回來後以一副專家的口吻説道：「很好，完全是典型的退化表現，我是説，依照那些圖畫來看。」

「你覺得以行為退化來稱呼那位年輕人，恰當嗎？」維拉克先生低喃説道。

「沒錯，科學界就是會這麼稱呼他。」奧斯朋回應：「看他耳朵的外觀就知道了，如果你拜讀過龍布羅梭的……」

卡爾·楊特打斷奧斯朋的話。

「龍布羅梭是傻子，對他而言，罪犯就是囚犯。將罪犯送入大牢的人，又是什麼？犯罪是什麼意思，他懂嗎？他只是個靠觀察窮苦倒楣鬼的耳朵和牙齒賺錢的笨蛋。牙齒和耳朵外觀能當作罪犯的記號嗎？那麼更能用來標示罪犯的法律，又要怎麼説？法律的同義詞就是燒得燙紅的烙鐵，這是豐衣足食而無法保護自己的人所發

明的招數，免得抵擋不了挨餓之人的攻擊。你難道沒聞過也沒聽過人皮灼傷的氣味和聲音嗎？罪犯就是這樣產生的。」

P. 35

不過，鼎鼎大名的「恐怖分子」卡爾·楊特，只會説大話而已。他從不付諸行動，甚至不是個能夠公開演講的人才。

史提夫聽到卡爾·楊特説的話後，即起身離開廚房。因為受到驚嚇，他沒拿好畫紙而掉落地上，以驚恐的眼神凝視著這位年邁恐怖分子。史提夫心裡很清楚，燙熱的烙鐵烙印在皮膚上一定非常痛，他嚇得瞠目結舌。

卡爾·楊特説：「你知道我會怎麼形容現在的經濟運作方式嗎？這是人

吃人的時代，他們就是這樣子！靠著人民的血肉，餵飽自己的貪婪。」

史提夫的眼睛瞪得更大，更加害怕起來。

這場會面很快就結束，大家紛紛離去。

維拉克先生對這群朋友不甚滿意。如果要以瓦拉迪莫先生製造暴動的想法來看，他們是無用之徒。但店裡現在生意慘澹，他很需要大使館這筆收入。

工作

• 維拉克先生的主要工作是什麼？他的第二份工作是什麼？他為什麼需要兩份工作？
• 你認識的人裡面，有多少人只做一份工作而已？

P. 36

維拉克先生關門時，發現史提夫仍在廚房裡。他看到史提夫時很驚訝，卻不知該跟他説些什麼，因此不發一語，就讓史提夫留在廚房裡。

溫妮在睡覺，他將溫妮叫起來，説道：「史提夫在樓下，我不知該拿他怎麼辦。」

她馬上起床，前往廚房。過一會兒回房後，她説史提夫非常焦躁不安。

「那孩子聽見太多你們講的話了。

他一直在哭叫自己偷聽到什麼吃人肉、喝人血的事。他不應該聽到你朋友的言論，他信以為真，很難受。」

維拉克先生沒有任何表示。

史提夫

• 史提夫為什麼會對每件事情信以為真呢？
• 你是否有時聽到別人的言論，卻不甚理解他們的意思呢？

4. 教授

P. 37

過了幾天，奧斯朋於午後前往席勒諾斯餐廳，坐在一張小型餐桌桌邊。他想和一位小個頭、戴著眼鏡、衣服又髒又舊的老人交談。人稱「教授」的這名老人，一副不太想説話的樣子，讓奧斯朋感到很不自在。

「在這裡坐很久了？」奧斯朋問道。

「一個多小時了吧。」

「那你可能還沒聽説今天的新聞，對吧？」

小老頭搖搖頭，看起來對於新聞內容不感好奇。

「是不是有人向你討東西，你就會給？」奧斯朋問道。

「我一向不拒絕別人。」

「萬一是警方派來的間諜，跟你要

121

貨呢？這樣他們手中就會握有逮補你的證據。」

「什麼證據？無照進行爆裂物交易嗎？我覺得他們不想逮補我，這我很清楚。」

「怎麼說？」奧斯朋問道。

P. 39

「他們心知肚明，我身上一直都會帶上一些貨。」他摸了一下胸前的外套。「我永遠不會被逮補。警察大人又不想當英雄。」

「他們不必要是英雄，他們只需要有一名員警，對於你口袋裡裝著足以將你自己和很多人炸成碎片的爆裂物一無所知即可。」奧斯朋回答。

「我可沒說過自己死不了，但那不算是逮補。總之，他們都知道我可以在幾秒內引爆炸彈。」

奧斯朋環顧餐廳四周一會兒。

「你的炸彈足以摧毀這間餐廳，把裡面的人都炸死。」

「這要具備意志堅定的人格特質，但這樣的人很少。」老人接續說道：「警方知道我是這種人，他們知道我不怕死，也不怕殺害很多人。這就是我比警方強大又占上風的一點。」

「警方也有這類性格特質的人。」奧斯朋說道。

「也許吧，但他們的性格特質是建立在中產階級的道德觀，而我是不受任何事物的拘束。他們得考慮到生活，但生活複雜，而且處處遭逢困境。可是我只需要思考死亡，簡單而無所畏懼，因此我擁有比誰都強大的優勢。」

P. 40

「我恐怕要挑戰你的想法。」奧斯朋說道：「今天早上有炸彈客在格林威治公園自爆。」

奧斯朋從口袋裡拿出一份報紙。

「你看，『格林威治公園的炸彈攻擊事件』。目前似乎沒有什麼線索。早上十一點半還在起大霧，公園樹下就炸出一個大洞，炸彈客的屍塊四散。我是不懂這個攻擊事件的目的，但恐怕會對我們造成負面影響。」

兩人靜默不語，奧斯朋終於再次開口。

「你最近是不是給了誰炸彈？一旦警方開竅，就會在你引爆貨品之前就對你格殺勿論。」

「沒錯。」老人認同這個說法，「但那不正是我們想達到的目的嗎？我們希望警方忘記自己得遵守規則和法律，當警方開始在街頭上掃射我們的時候，我反而開心，大眾也會高興。這表示他們的道德觀開始瓦解，也是我們贏得勝利的起步。這是我們應該要達成的目標。」

「今天早上的攻擊事件，炸彈到底是不是來自你這裡？我們倫敦小組完全不知情，你可以描述一下炸彈客的樣子嗎？」奧斯朋問道。

「可以，就一個名字：維拉克。」

P. 41

奧斯朋震驚地往後靠在椅背。
「維拉克！不可能。」

炸彈

• 誰該為炸彈攻擊事件負責？
• 我們如何得知此事？
• 炸彈在哪裡引爆？
• 罹難者有誰？

「據我所知，他是倫敦小組的重要成員。」

「是重要沒錯，不，倒也未必，應該說他的用處大於他的重要性。他缺乏想法，庸庸碌碌。他唯一的才能就是懂得躲避警方的注意力，因為他是有家室的人。他有沒有向你透露他的意圖？」奧斯朋說道。

P. 42

「他說要利用攻擊建物來達到殺雞儆猴的效果。」教授說道。

「你想到底發生什麼事了？」奧斯朋問道。

「我不知道。他啟動引爆裝置後，計時器就開始二十分鐘的倒數。如果要讓炸彈提早引爆，只需要重擊炸彈即可。所以，他要嘛拖太久而擺脫不了炸彈，要嘛不小心摔到炸彈，但只有笨蛋會這麼做。」

奧斯朋坐在椅子上思考著。警方可能已經在維拉克的商店佈下天羅地網，因此他不想去那裡。但倘若如報紙所述，炸彈客已被炸得支離破碎，身分難以辨識，警方不會有什麼特別的理由去監視維拉克的商店。

「我很納悶我現在該怎麼做。」奧斯朋低喃著。

「盡可能從他太太那裡套話，他們一定有收到一筆錢。」教授說道。

奧斯朋

• 他接下來會怎麼行動？

5. 總督察希特

P. 43

總督察希特過了糟糕的一天。首先，他的部門在當天早上接獲來自格林威治的電報。他心想：「我的運氣就是這麼差，不到一個星期之前，我才跟內政部長報告過，絕對沒有無政府主義者要在倫敦鬧事。」

而且他飢腸轆轆，卻還得到醫院查看屍體。他一到醫院就胃口盡失，實在不習慣這麼近距離查看肢離破碎的人類遺體。當另一名警官掀起蓋屍布時，他十分震驚，眼前的景象是燒焦又佈滿血跡的破爛衣物，混雜著看似獅子飽餐後所吃剩的肉塊。這一整天，他無法下嚥任何食物。

「嫌犯的遺體都在這裡，一點也沒少。」警官說道，開始闡述過程，「我是爆炸發生後，第一個抵達現場的人。」他解說著：「我盤查的老太太說，她看見兩名男子走出車站。她不確定這兩人是不是一夥的。她說一個男子體型胖碩，另一個男子則是金髮又瘦弱，而且一手拿著顏色醒目的金屬罐。你看，他就躺在這裡，金髮又瘦弱，看看那隻腳。我先撿起他的腳，再陸續撿拾他的屍塊，因為炸得到處都是，我們得使用鏟子。」

P. 45

警官停頓了一下，說道：「他大概是被樹根絆倒，他帶著的那顆炸彈，就這麼的在他胸膛下方爆炸了。」

總督察好不容易克服想吐的感覺，伸手拿起沾上最少血漬的布。這是一塊長條型的窄版絲絨布，上頭還連著一大片三角形的深藍色布料。

「那位老太太有注意到絲絨布料的領口，她告訴我們，那人穿著絲絨布料領口的深藍色大衣。」警官說道。

總督察走到窗邊，仔細查看這塊藍布。他快速甩動，讓藍布脫離絲絨布後就放入他的口袋，然後轉身將絲絨布領口放回驗屍桌上。

「蓋起來吧。」他對一位警官如是說，隨即快步離去。

總督察回到警局後，直奔助理警務處長的辦公室。

爆炸事件

• 是誰身上帶著炸彈？
• 這個人發生了什麼事？在描述此人經歷的文字部分畫底線。

P. 46

「你是對的。」助理警務處長說道：「調查報告已經出爐，我們很清楚每個倫敦無政府主義分子身在何處。他們並未犯下這起罪行，這件事與他們無關。」

總督察則告知來龍去脈，並闡述他目前的推論和觀察。

他說道：「在我看來，那兩名男子一起抵達之後，在距離皇家天文台圍牆的一百碼處就分道揚鑣。當時的霧雖然不濃，卻很可能掩飾了體型胖碩的男子，讓他在不被發現的情況下離開公園。看來是他帶著小個子的男子前往引爆地點，然後將他留在那裡自行完成任務。」

「你有搜捕那名胖碩男子嗎？」助理警務處長問道。

總督察提及了車站名稱，說道：「長官，他們就是從那裡而來。負責在迷宮山車站幫忙回收車票的行李員，記得那兩名符合描述的男子。胖碩男子從三等車廂出來，手上拿著醒目的金屬罐。在月台的時候，他將金屬罐交給跟在後頭的金髮年輕男子。所有描述都符合格林威治警官盤查老太太的證詞。」

P. 47

助理警務處長認為這兩名男子與攻擊事件無關，這只是老太太口說無憑的故事。

「爆炸現場有很多金屬罐碎片，這是很好的佐證。」總督察說道。

「所以，這兩名男子來自鄉下小車站。」助理警務處長接著說：「從那個地方來的兩名外來無政府主義分子，我認為不太可能吧。」

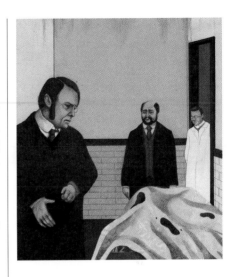

「話是沒錯，助理處長，但是麥可利斯就待在那一區的農莊裡。」

6. 麥可利斯

P. 48

麥可利斯出獄後，一名年邁貴婦決定伸出援手，將她名下的一座鄉間農莊送給麥可利斯。這名貴婦在助理警務處長夫人的交際圈裡，算是極具影響力的重要人物。

麥可利斯被判無期徒刑，罪名是與他人同謀攔阻警車劫囚。當時一名員警不慎遇害，留下太太與三名年幼孩子，這起事件讓社會大眾為之震驚。當時年輕纖瘦的麥可利斯，雖然與殺害員警一事無關，但他在接受審判時說道：「那名員警的殉職，讓我非常難過。對於無法救出囚犯一事，我同樣感到遺憾又傷心。」

因此，社會大眾恨他入骨，當他入獄十五年後假釋出獄，報章雜誌都是他的新聞。

一天傍晚，一名重要的訪客帶麥可利斯前往那名貴婦的宅邸。雖然他在闡述自己社會正義方面的遠大抱負時，詞不達意，但他的熱忱與樂觀卻讓貴婦印象深刻。她認為麥可利斯並非危險份子，因此決定照顧他。

P. 50

助理警務處長曾經從太太那裡聽到那位貴婦對麥可利斯的評價，她說麥可利斯或許是個感情用事、有點狂妄的人，但絕對不會刻意傷害任何人。因此，當總督察提起麥可利斯或許涉及這起爆炸事件時，助理警務處長才意識到整件事的危險。

「麥可利斯現在是假釋狀態。」助理警務處長心想：「如果我們逮捕他，警方會讓他回牢服完殘刑。他會在獄中因身上肥油窒息而死，而我太太永遠都不會原諒我。」

「你有辦法找到麥可利斯和這起案件的關聯性嗎？」他問道。

總督察希特說道：「助理處長，我們已經握有將矛頭指向他的充足情報。反正像他那樣的人，也不應該逍遙法外。」

「你一定要找到確鑿的證據。」助理警務處長回話。

「要找到對他不利的充足證據，一點都不難，」總督察希特說道：「這一點您可以相信我，長官。」

助理警務處長越來越不悅。

他心想：「希特既然對麥可利斯這麼反感，也可能會設法與我作對。」

「某些理由讓我認為，你踏進我辦公室時，心裡想的並不是麥可利斯。」助理警務處長說道。

「長官，您有理由認為？」總督察希特說道。

P. 51

「沒錯，我有我的理由。如果麥可利斯真的是嫌犯，為什麼你沒有私下或是派你的手下先到他的農莊去調查？」助理警務處長說道。

「長官，您覺得我沒有盡到分內職責嗎？」總督察問道。

「我不是這個意思。」助理警務處長以一副「你明知故問」的表情回應。他接著說：「你的能力無庸置疑，但是你到底能找到什麼對麥可利斯不利的具體證據？我的意思是，除了那兩名嫌犯從距離麥可利斯所處鄉村三英里內的火車站上車以外，還有什麼證據？」

「長官，像他那種人，這樣的線索就足以讓我們朝這個方向去偵查。」總督察說道。

「你覺得麥可利斯涉及炸彈前置作

業嗎？」助理警務處長問道。

「我覺得沒有。但很明顯的是，他與這起攻擊有某種程度的關聯，他可是列在我們『危險分子』名單上的。」

總督察很確定麥可利斯一定多少知情，只是知道得不多，甚至可能知道的比「教授」還少。但是，除非打破某些規則，否則很難逮捕「教授」。不過，這樣的遊戲規則可不會保護麥可利斯。

P. 52

遊戲規則

• 所謂的「遊戲」是什麼呢？又是怎麼樣的規則呢？請和朋友一起討論。

「總督察，說說你在格林威治調查出了什麼吧。」

「我查到一個地址。」總督察說道，然後從他的口袋掏出用墨水寫著「貝瑞特街 32 號」的一塊深藍色布料。「這塊布來自死者身上穿的大衣。當然，我們不清楚大衣是否為死者擁有，但這是一家商店的地址，老闆是維拉克先生。」

他們兩人對看了一眼。

總督察接著說：「當然，我們警局並沒有維拉克的官方資料，因為他是我私下找的線人。我的一名法國警察朋友告訴我，維拉克是某大使館的間諜。」

「原來如此。那好吧，你和這位大使館間諜私下聯絡多久了？」

「我大概七年多前第一次見到他，當時有兩名皇室成員和財政大臣到這裡巡視。維拉克給了我一條十分重要的情報，就是兩名皇室成員可能會受到攻擊。」

「那你後來怎麼處理？」助理警務處長問道。

P. 53

「一天傍晚，我前往他的商店。他說自己已婚，只求繼續做小本生意餬口。他所做的生意不完全合法，因此我承諾他，只要他別過分違法，警方就會對他睜一隻眼閉一隻眼。」

「那麼他給了你哪些好處，來換得你的保護？」

「情報。我會寄給他未署名的簡短留言，他也以相同方法寄回到我的私

人地址。在我看來，他對於這起攻擊事件毫不知情。」

「那麼你要怎麼解釋這塊布？」助理警務處長邊說邊指著寫有維拉克地址的那塊布。

「就我目前所知，解釋不了。我認為涉入最深的人，還是麥可利斯。」

「逃離公園的那名男子該怎麼解釋？」

「他大概早已逍遙法外。」總督察說道。

「總督察，找到他，明天一早再來向我匯報進度。」

總督察一離開，助理警務處長也離開了警局。

7. 助理警務處長

P. 54

助理警務處長進入一棟公共大樓，要求晉見內政部長。他被帶入一間寬敞廳室，而人高馬大的內政部長伊瑟瑞德就站在裡面。

內政部長說道：「請告訴我，這是不是連續爆炸事件的開端而已。不用交代細節，我沒時間聽。」

「我認為不是，不過這起事件並非一般的無政府主義暴行，我就是為了這個原因而來的。」

「非常好，繼續說下去，不用交代細節。」

助理警務處長把他和總督察希特的談話內容，告訴了內政部長：「這件案子的背後暗潮洶湧，我們要格外留意。」

「你的想法大體上是什麼？簡單說就好，不用講得太詳細。」

「祕密間諜這種事是不能容忍的，他們會使原先要對抗的邪惡之事更加危險。很明顯，間諜會編撰假情報。在政治與革新行動方面，專業間諜非常有可能自行假造『事實』，造成某方刻意包裝不實訊息，將恐慌、草率上路的法律與盲目的仇恨加諸於對立的另一方。因此，這個案件須維持保密狀態，而且我覺得應該先找您商量才對。」

P. 56

「我很欣慰還有警察覺得內政部長是可信任的對象。你盡量說得簡短。」

「伊瑟瑞德部長，我不會贅述細節。炸彈客大衣上的地址是極為重要的線索，只要找到這項證據的合理解釋，就能釐清案件的真相。我不希望讓希特繼續追查本案，我期盼能親自找出合理的解釋，也就是讓我前往貝瑞特街的這間商店，見見這位鼎鼎大名的祕密間諜。」

「為什麼不讓希特去處理？」

「因為他認為自己的職責就是盡可能將知名的無政府主義分子關入大

牢，即使未掌握確切證據也無妨，而不是深究檯面下的內幕。他是傑出的警官，但這起案件非同小可。況且，我不希望辦案時綁手綁腳，我想擁有高於一般督察的權限。我不會放過這個維拉克，嚇唬他並非難事，他一定能做出解釋。但我需要您的許可，讓我承諾他的人身安全無虞。」

希特

• 希特想怎麼做？為什麼？

P. 57

「當然沒問題，竭盡所能的挖掘線索，用你自己的方式去追查吧。」內政部長說道。

「我會馬上著手處理。」助理警務處長說道。

「盡快向我回報進度。」內政部長說道。

助理警務處長回到辦公室更換衣服，並派人傳訊給他的夫人。他們當晚本來要赴約那位照顧麥可利斯的貴婦所舉辦的晚宴，因此他請夫人替他無法出席一事道歉，然後就動身前往貝瑞特街了。

助理警務處長

• 他認為誰該為這起案件負責？
• 他不想逮捕誰？為什麼？
• 貴婦是何人？請與朋友討論。

8. 史提夫

P. 58

在維拉克夫人的母親和亡夫的友人們堅決要求之後，終於在一家養老院得到容身之處，但這個消息讓她的女兒很吃驚。

「您為什麼這麼做？」女兒問道。溫妮其實不想知道全部的實情，所以在母親開口之前，她先問：「另外，母親您是怎麼辦到的？」

「親愛的，就是透過你那可憐爸爸的朋友們。」母親說道。

母親不想透露她的用意。母親之所以想離開，是因為她知道維拉克先生是個好丈夫，只是她不確定能持續多久。她覺得自己跟他們住，可能會更快把維拉克的好脾氣磨掉了，而且她也想讓史提夫能夠完全依賴維拉克先生，他才會永遠照顧這個可憐的孩子。因此，為了確保維拉克先生能負責兒子的未來，她選擇離開家人。

要接送到養老院的馬車抵達時，溫妮的母親很驚訝，因為映入眼簾的是一匹瘦弱的病馬，緩緩拖著輪子顛簸的車廂，而馬伕的一隻手掌是鐵勾義肢。警察再三向她保證：「我認識這位馬伕。」他說道：「他二十年來都沒有出過車禍。」

P. 60

溫妮和母親坐進車廂，史提夫則爬上車廂外的馬伕座。由於馬匹行進速度極慢，因此花了很久的時間才抵達目的地。史提夫盯著馬看，變得越來越緊張。

史提夫終於開口：「不要用馬鞭，不可以。」他結巴地說：「馬會痛。」

「不可以用馬鞭？」馬伕說道，隨即揮動馬鞭，因為他還得掙錢。

史提夫突然跳下馬伕座，引起街上騷動。

「史提夫！立刻上來馬伕座，別再跳下去了。」

「不要，不要。走路，一定要走路。」

溫妮好不容易說服他上來馬伕座坐好。他們終於抵達養老院，溫妮和母親先進屋，史提夫則幫忙將行李搬進去。他出來之後，仍看著那匹可憐的馬。此時馬伕走向他。

馬伕說：「牠沒有跛腳，也不會痛。坐在牠後面，駕車到凌晨三、四點，你覺得是很輕鬆的事嗎？我又冷又餓，只為了賺錢，你這酒鬼。」

史提夫仍盯著馬看。

他說道：「我是值夜班的馬伕，我太太和四個孩子都在家等我，日子不好過啊。」

P. 61

史提夫的臉龐抽搐著，然後一如往常的以簡單字句來表達他的感受。「很糟糕！很糟糕！」

「對馬刻薄就算了，沒想到對我這樣的可憐人更刻薄。」馬伕說道。

「可憐！可憐！」史提夫一邊結巴，一邊將雙手緊緊塞入口袋。他說

不出話來，他想起被父親歐打而躲在黑暗角落，感到害怕、疼痛、難堪的那些時光。他的姊姊總是會過來抱住他，一起躺在床上，讓他感到天堂般的安寧與慰藉。他想用溫妮安慰他的方式，來安慰那匹馬和馬伕，但他知道自己做不到。

溫妮離開養老院後，便和史提夫一起搭公車。他們看見馬車停在一家酒吧外，溫妮一眼就認出來。

「可憐的馬兒！」她說道。

「可憐！可憐！」史提夫回應道：「車伕也可憐，他自己跟我說的。真遺憾！」

可憐的車伕要靠鞭打可憐的馬，才養得起家裡可憐的孩子，他簡短幾個字，說出他對世道不公的震驚。史提夫很清楚挨打的感覺。

世道不公

• 你認同史提夫的想法嗎？
• 你也認同溫妮的想法嗎？
  請在課堂上討論。

9. 暴行

P. 62

維拉克先生很鬱悶。他在前往歐洲之前，就已經不太開心。十天後他回國，憂愁仍如影隨形。

維拉克夫人告訴丈夫，史提夫一直悶悶不樂。

「都是因為母親離開了我們。」她說。

維拉克先生不是真的在聽，不過當他說要出門的時候，太太要他帶史提夫一起去。

「他可能會跟不上我的腳步，然後在大街上迷路。」維拉克先生說道。

「我會確保他跟緊。」太太說道。

「好，那就讓他一起來吧。」

接下來幾天，維拉克先生並不介意帶著史提夫。他準備出門散步時，會用一種狀似呼喚愛犬的方式叫喊史提夫。這一天，他告訴太太，他想將史提夫送出城一陣子。

「麥可利斯住在鄉間的一座小農莊，他願意讓史提夫下榻。」他說道：「那裡不會有訪客和閒話，對史提夫而言未嘗不是件好事。」

溫妮同意了，因此維拉克先生隔天就帶史提夫前往鄉下，讓他住在麥可利斯家。

P. 63

在格林威治公園炸彈攻擊未遂事件的那天，維拉克先生一大早就出門，溫妮則整天獨自待在家裡。她沒有看報紙，當丈夫於黃昏時分回來時，她正坐在店裡的櫃台後方。

「今天真難熬。」她說道：「你有去看史提夫嗎？」

「沒有！我沒去。」維拉克先生說完就進屋內。

她過了一會兒才跟上去，想幫丈夫準備晚餐。維拉克先生就坐在沙發上，他的牙齒不由自主的打顫，身體也在發抖。

溫妮看了雖然擔心，但她還是先擺好晚餐餐具。

「你今天去哪裡了？」她問道。

「沒去哪裡。」維拉克先生回話：「我去了銀行。」

「為什麼？」

「把錢都領出來。」

「所有的錢？為什麼要這麼做？」

「可能很快就用得到。」

「我不懂你的意思。」太太說道。

「你知道你可以信任我吧。」維拉克先生說。

「是啊，我信任你。」她說道，一邊擺了兩個餐盤，拿了麵包、奶油、一點牛肉和一把切肉刀與叉子，然後叫丈夫上桌吃飯。丈夫就坐在對面。

P. 64

他的雙眼佈滿血絲，滿臉通紅，整個頭髮亂七八糟。溫妮以為他生病了。他喝了三杯茶後卻未進食，而是開始談起移民至西班牙或加州的事。溫妮看得出來，維拉克先生目前的身心狀態都不像平常的他。

「你感冒了。」她說道。

這時，店門鈴響起。維拉克先生不甘願地起身去見顧客。他們待在店裡滿長的時間。

維拉克先生返回後，臉色蒼白。

「怎麼了？」溫妮問道。

她看到顧客還在店裡，但認不出是誰，因為助理警務處長既不是常客，也不是認識的朋友。

「我得出門一趟。」維拉克先生說。

「那你領出來的錢怎麼辦？」她問道：「在你口袋裡嗎？我覺得比較安全的做法是......」

「錢！對，對，當然。都在這裡。」他將所有的錢交給溫妮，然後和那位陌生顧客離開。

她將錢藏在口袋時，門鈴再次響起。一名男子走進來，維拉克夫人記得曾經看過他。

「維拉克夫人，你丈夫在家嗎？」他問道。

總督察希特私下前來拜訪維拉克先生，希望能從他口中套出可以誣陷麥可利斯的情報。

P. 66

「他剛和一名陌生人離開了。」溫妮說道。總督察可從她的描述判斷出，那名陌生人就是助理警務處長。「我就知道！」他心想。然後他告訴溫妮那人的來歷，並詢問溫妮剛剛發生了什麼事。

他很訝異，溫妮竟然不知道格林威治爆炸事件。

「我們認為我們找到了......一件被偷的大衣。」他說道：「這件大衣裡縫

有一片標籤，標籤上用墨水寫著你們的地址。」

「那是我弟弟的大衣。」

「你弟在哪裡？我可以見他嗎？」

「他不在。他一直待在鄉下的一個朋友家裡。」

「那個朋友叫什麼名字？」

「麥可利斯。」維拉克夫人説道。

「啊！那你弟弟長什麼樣子？體型胖碩和深髮色？」

「喔不，那一定是小偷的樣子。史提夫體型瘦弱又是金髮，是我將地址標籤縫在大衣裡，以免他迷路的，因為他常常迷路。」

「那表示我今天早上查看的遺體，就是維拉克夫人的弟弟！」總督察心中頓時恍然大悟。「但那表示『另一名男子』就是維拉克啊！」

恍然大悟

• 總督察希特領悟到什麼？

P. 67

就在這時候，維拉克先生回家了。

他見到總督察希特，劈頭就問：「你在這裡做什麼？」

總督察回答：「我來找你談一談。」

他們走到後側休息室，維拉克夫人則恍惚的呆坐著。但他們忘了把門關好，因此她聽到總督察希特説：「維拉克，你就是逃逸的另一名男子。目擊者説看見兩名男子進入公園，我們認為你的小舅子被樹根絆倒，將自己炸得粉碎。到處混雜著屍塊、沙礫、衣服和骨頭，他們還得用鏟子才能把遺體都搜集起來。」

「你聽好，那個孩子智能不足，又不用負法律責任，他就算被逮捕，也不會被押入大牢。最糟的情況不過是被送進收容所。」維拉克説道。

溫妮

• 溫妮聽到了什麼？
• 「被絆倒」的男子是誰？
• 他發生什麼事？
• 維拉克對這個男子有何評價？
• 你覺得溫妮會有何感受？

P. 68

總督察希特察覺到，維拉克先生坦白的自首説詞會壞事。不只會揭露「教授」暗地進行的活動與造成各種問題，而且還沒辦法誣陷麥可利斯，他不希望走到這樣的局面。

「我建議你趁還可以的時候，盡快消失。」總督察說道。

「我希望你今晚就能帶我離開。」維拉克先生一邊說，一邊往太太待著的前頭店面看去。

「我知道。」總督察說道：「但我做不到。」他開門走向店面離去。

仍坐在櫃台後方的維拉克夫人雙手掩面，未直視總督察。她將婚戒取下，丟進垃圾桶。

垃圾桶

- 溫妮將什麼物品丟到垃圾桶？
- 為什麼？
- 你覺得她接下來會怎麼做？

10. 伊瑟瑞德部長

P. 70

助理警務處長離開貝瑞特街，直接前往西敏寺，準備向內政部長伊瑟瑞德匯報他所得到的線索。部長立刻接見他。

他表示，被罪惡感壓得喘不過氣的維拉克有意自首。

「你追查到什麼事？」伊瑟瑞德部長問道。

「炸彈客是維拉克的小舅子，是一名智力發展遲緩的年輕人。他的死是一場意外，麥可利斯和整起事件毫無干係，但耐人尋味的是維拉克為什麼要籌畫這起攻擊暴行。」

助理警務處長繼續報告說，他知道維拉克和瓦拉迪莫先生會晤的事。「維拉克心生恐懼。我想他昏了頭，深信大使館的人有能耐將他祕密間諜的身分昭告天下。我認為他並不是難以教化的罪犯。」

「那你對他做了哪些處置？」

P. 72

「伊瑟瑞德部長，他似乎很焦慮的急著回去店裡找他太太，所以我放了他。他不會就此逃逸，因為他得替夥伴的安危著想。目前為止，尚無任何人知道他涉嫌這個案件，但他如果試圖逃跑……」

「很好。你還有什麼事要告訴我的嗎？」

「伊瑟瑞德部長，我想沒有了，除非您要我述說細節……」

「不用了，不用說細節。我今晚會和檢察總長討論這起事件，明天早上再來見我。你可以走了。」

11. 維拉克夫婦

P. 73

在貝瑞特街的公寓裡，維拉克先生不知所措，也不知該如何面對太

太。在他的攻擊計畫裡，不會有人受傷，即使有，也決不會是史提夫。對他而言，史提夫喪生所帶來的問題，比他在世時更加麻煩。而他萬萬沒想到的是，太太居然會在史提夫的大衣裡縫上地址標籤。

他吃了仍擺放在餐桌上的牛肉。「我不是有意要讓他受到傷害。」他說。

溫妮不願和他交談。他用盡各種方式來和她溝通：他指責總督察希特害她傷心；他希望溫妮能想想未來；他告訴溫妮，在他坐牢期間，他需要她幫忙管店；甚至說出警方會找上門都是她的錯，因為是她把地址縫在大衣裡，但他原諒她。

P. 74

最後，他怪到瓦拉迪莫先生身上：「你無法想像我從大使館回來後承受的所有壓力；我一直憂心忡忡，有很多次我都想就此逃到國外，但我還是為了你留下來。」

推卸責任

- 維拉克將一切都怪在誰身上？
- 你對維拉克這個人有何感想？
- 你認識總是怨天尤人的人嗎？請和朋友討論。

溫妮完全聽不進去。她腦海裡浮現的是，在短租公寓的空蕩頂樓，拿著一根蠟燭、帶著史提夫回床睡覺的畫面。她回憶起幫史提夫梳頭更衣的情景；她的年紀沒有大史提夫多少，但小時候的她多了點勇氣，像個小大人般的安慰嬌小又容易受到驚嚇的小弟。她彷彿又看見當年為了幫弟弟擋住父親的拳腳而被揮到頭、為了躲避暴怒父親而緊關房門卻很快被踹開的景象。而火爆父親的憤怒言語，似乎仍迴盪耳邊。

她還想起與一名年輕人陷入熱戀的過去。他想娶她，但經濟拮据只夠小倆口過活，完全無法負擔史提夫的生活。因此，她為了確保史提夫的生活無虞，才決定嫁給維拉克先生。

維拉克先生仍滔滔不絕說著他的隱憂。「溫妮，清醒一點。」他說道：「看著我。」

回憶

- 溫妮的腦海裡想起何人？
- 她為何嫁給維拉克先生？

P. 76

「只要我還活著的一天，我就不想見到你。」她言盡於此。

然後她起身上樓，換裝下樓準備出門。

「現在是八點二十五分，溫妮。你今晚還是待在家裡，把帽子脫掉，我不能讓你出去。」他說道，然後舒服的坐在沙發上。他說：「我真的希望能忘掉格林威治公園的事。」

公園這幾個字眼，讓溫妮想起總督察希特告訴她的爆炸細節，一切如跑馬燈般閃過她眼前：格林威治公園，灰飛煙滅的枝葉沙礫、四散的屍塊與碎骨；他們要用鏟子搜集所有的遺骸。她站在沙發旁，開始顫抖。

「溫妮，過來。」他說道。

她往沙發走去，經過餐桌時，順手拿起切肉刀。維拉克先生看見她拿刀的舉動，還來不及反應，切肉刀就已深深插入他的胸膛。

12. 奧斯朋

P. 77

溫妮·維拉克過了一會兒才回神察覺自己鑄下大錯，當她看見鮮血時，想到自己只有一個下場：絞刑。她記得報紙報導過監獄的處決方式。官員都會在場見證犯人被吊死，而「絞刑架離地的高度有十四英尺」。

一想到落下絞刑架後，頭部因為絞勒力道而與肩膀分離的畫面，她就不禁想嘔吐。不！決不能發生這樣的事，她決定在警方找到她之前，到橋邊投河自盡。

她拉下帽子的網紗後離家。走在街上令她恐懼，彷彿是邁向絞刑或投河自盡之路。她全身無力，舉步艱難，甚至需要扶著街燈柱子才能避免跌倒。

「我在明天早上之前，一定到不了河邊，那邊太遠了。」她絕望的想著。

P. 79

她穩住自己，黑色網紗下的呼吸十分沉重，腦海又出現「絞刑架離地的高度有十四英尺」的字句。

她突然想到潛逃出境，謀殺案的兇手都是逃到國外，去西班牙或加州都好。但是，對她而言都只是個地名，因為她沒有門路到達任何地方。謀殺案兇手有朋友、靠關係、有幫手，而且消息靈通。但她一無所有，

完全孤單無援。

她開始踉蹌走著。一抬頭，便看見一名男子貼近她的網紗細瞧。奧斯朋沒認出她，以為是個喝醉的婦人。

「奧斯朋先生！」她說道。

「維拉克夫人！」他回話。

奧斯朋思考了一天：「教授」製造了一枚炸彈交給維拉克；炸彈在格林威治公園引爆後，炸死身帶炸彈的男子；所以維拉克已經身亡。奧斯朋整天下來，猶豫不決是否該去看看維拉克的遺孀。錢一定放在某處，但又擔心警方已經在監視他們的住所。可是像維拉克夫人這樣的女子，又不可能在夜晚獨自出門還喝醉，但他還是決定碰運氣試探一下。

「我遠遠就認出你了。」奧斯朋謊稱：「我擔心你會跌倒。」

「你是要來店裡嗎？」她突然看見一絲希望，也許她未如想像中的孤單。

P. 80

「是的，我一看到晚報新聞就決定過來。」奧斯朋急切的解釋：「我決定來找你，我想幫助你，因為打從第一次見到你，我就愛上你了。」

奧斯朋算計著，沒有女人抵擋得了這種說法。但他不知道的是，維拉克夫人的反應完全出於自我保護的本能。因為對她而言，說謊的奧斯朋剛好給了她一線生機。

「我也是這麼想的。」她說道。

「像你這樣的女子，我沒辦法再隱瞞對你的愛慕之情。」他繼續胡謅，卻一邊想著商店的資產總額和維拉克先生銀行帳戶的存款。「但你一直很冷漠，我以為你愛的是他……」

「愛他？」維拉克夫人怒氣沖沖地說道：「愛他？我當時只是個年輕女孩。我身心俱疲，母親和弟弟都要依賴我。我還能怎麼辦？我嫁給他，謹守婦道七年。但你知道他的真面目嗎？他簡直是個惡魔！」

「我都不知情。」奧斯朋說道，一邊納悶她到底在說什麼，想套出實情。「我懂，但他已經死了。」

「既然你猜到他已經死了。」她說道：「那你也應該猜得到我付出了什麼代價。」

P. 81

奧斯朋開始思考：他知道身亡的炸彈客是維拉克，但維拉克夫人怎麼會知情？警方尚無法辨識遺體的身分，消息都還沒見報。她是否涉入攻擊事件？為什麼對死去的丈夫如此氣憤？難道她丈夫是自殺身亡，在他們兩人之中，惡魔指的並非維拉克？

誰才是惡魔？

- 奧斯朋忽略了什麼訊息？
  請與朋友討論。

「你一開始是怎麼聽說整件事？」他問道。

「警方告訴我的。一個叫希特的總督察來店裡，他說警方還得用鏟子搜集遺骸！」

「警方已經來過了？總督察希特做了什麼處置？」

「什麼都沒做就走了。警方和維拉克那傢伙是同一夥的，還有另一個人來，也許是大使館的人。」

奧斯朋這時震驚連連，幾乎要崩潰。

「大使館！什麼大使館？」

「在切舍姆廣場那裡，是哪都一樣，別問我。」她說道。

P. 82

接下來，她告訴奧斯朋她要逃到

歐洲，並要他一道走。對奧斯朋而言，整件事變得太複雜，但他心裡還是不停覬覦著維拉克的財產。他告訴溫妮，火車班次要等到早上才有，他可以幫她找找短租公寓的房間，但是他沒錢付租金或車票費用。

「我的錢夠用。」

「你有多少錢？」

「我有全部的銀行存款，他交給我了。救救我吧！將我藏起來。別讓他們抓住我，否則你得先殺了我。」

奧斯朋越來越疑惑。

維拉克夫人

- 她為什麼要跟奧斯朋打交道？
- 奧斯朋為什麼讓她感到「一線生機」？請參閱第 79 頁。

「你到底在怕什麼？」他突然想起：南安普敦開往法國聖馬洛的客船午夜出發，而倫敦通往南安普敦的最後一班火車時間是十點半。他們早上就能抵達法國。

「還有時間。」他説道：「我們會沒事的。」

但維拉克夫人開始回頭走向貝瑞特街。

P. 84

「我出來的時候忘了關店門。」她説道。

他無法理解她何必在乎店門，畢竟他們都要離開英格蘭了 …… 但他還是跟在她身後。

店門微開，後側休息室的燈仍亮著。

「我忘了熄燈！」維拉克夫人説道：「拜託你幫我進去熄燈，否則我會瘋掉。」

「存款都在哪裡？」他説道。

「在我身上！快點！快進去熄燈。」

燈光

• 維拉克夫人為什麼叫奧斯朋去熄燈？
• 你會想要藉由口述或示範的方式，來向別人透露事情嗎？為什麼？請與朋友討論。

奧斯朋進去休息室，看見維拉克先生靜靜的躺在沙發上休息。

他差點叫出來，但忍住了。這是怎麼回事，是他錯亂了，還是一場惡夢，抑或是對方設的陷阱？這對夫婦打算謀殺他嗎？為什麼？還有為什麼維拉克先生在裝睡？然後，他看見了鮮血，還有插在維拉克先生胸前的刀子。他馬上轉頭頻頻乾嘔。

P. 86

維拉克夫人走進店裡，喃喃自語：「我不會被吊死。」

奧斯朋熄了燈。他開始懷疑屋裡可能有其他人在，因此他走到前頭店面，將後側休息室的門鎖上。

「是你自己殺了他嗎？」他問道。

「對。」

「沒有人會相信的。」他説道。

他現在無從判斷這起難以置信的事件中，所有訊息的可信度，抑或可能發生的情況。他開始懼怕這個情緒激憤的女人，她到底想從他這裡得到什麼？她想告訴警方他也涉入這起謀殺案嗎？一切都沒有道理。

「他死前在睡覺嗎？」

「不是。」她説道：「他舒服地躺在沙發上，居然能夠在殺了我那親愛的弟弟後，還這麼怡然自得。我想就此離開，永遠不再見他。但他殺了我親愛的弟弟，還能面不改色的對我説『過來』。」

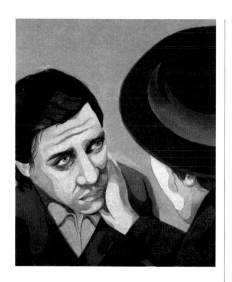

奧斯朋頓時恍然大悟：格林威治公園的死者是那名智力發展遲緩的年輕人。

現在他更加深對她的恐懼，退化者的姊姊，竟也表現出另一種退化模式── 犯下了謀殺罪。他被扯進去了，沒有人會相信溫妮殺害了她丈夫，而且只要他們還一起待在這個家，她就能想辦法推説他才是兇手。

他突然下定決心。

「我們快走，否則會趕不上火車。」

P. 87

他們搭馬車前往車站，奧斯朋一邊説明他的計畫。

「我們到達車站時，你一定要比我先走進車站，佯裝我們互不相識，因為警方可能會守在車站。你單獨搭車的話，會被當作一般老百姓。但警方認得我，和我走在一起，他們就猜得出你是逃逸的維拉克夫人。我會先去買票，經過你身旁時，將車票偷塞在你手中。然後你先前往女仕的頭等候車室，在那裡待到發車前的十分鐘。接下來你先走去月台，我會跟著你。對了，我現在需要那筆錢買車票。」

她將裝滿存款的小袋子交給他。

「你知道裡面有多少錢嗎？」他問。

「不知道，我沒有算。」

他們抵達車站後，奧斯朋跟在後面，一切按照計畫進行。他們各自搭上火車，在車廂裡碰面。

「去坐在車廂另一端的座位吧，親愛的，這樣比較安全。」奧斯朋説道。

她心懷感激地看著他：「我將用此生報答你！」

火車終於啟程。奧斯朋跨了兩大步穿越車廂，開了車門跳出車外。

火車離開車站時，他荷包滿滿地踏上回家的路，然後倒頭大睡。

P. 88

隔日，他買了一份報紙。一篇文章的結語寫著「沒有人能夠解開此瘋狂或絕望行為的謎團」，而文章斗大的標題為「女性乘客於開往法國的客船自縊」。

他癱軟無力放下報紙。這是一個全世界永遠解不開的謎題。而他只能日日買醉，借酒忘卻讓他畢生揮之不去的事情真相。

ANSWER KEY

Before Reading Activities

Pages 18-21

1 ⓐ 4　ⓑ 1　ⓒ 3　ⓓ 2

2 c, a, d, b

3 ⓐ 3　ⓑ 2　ⓒ 4　ⓓ 1

4 1. c　2. a　3. d　4. b

5 a. cab, whip　b. target
c. gallows, rope, drop
d. shovel, gravel

6 a. legal　b. trial　c. evidence
d. released　e. committed
f. gallows　g. suspect
h. investigate　i. guilt
j. parole　k. confesses
l. sentence　m. executions
n. incriminates　o. rope

While Reading Activities

Page 24

• Winnie Verloc, her mother and her brother Stevie.
• He has a job and another mysterious business.

Page 35

• His main job is his shop.
• He works with the Embassy.
• He needs the money.

Page 41

• Verloc.
• The Professor tells Ossipon.
• Greenwich Park.
• A man was killed.

Page 56

• Heat wants to arrest Michaelis because he thinks that he knows something about the bomb.

Page 57

• He doesn't know.
• He doesn't want Michaelis to be arrested because Michaelis is a friend of his wife's.

Page 66

• He realizes that Verloc was the second man at the bomb site.

Page 67

• She hears Verloc talking about the bomb. / Stevie. / He was killed. / He says he was half-witted and irresponsible.

Page 68

• Her wedding ring.
• Because she is disgusted by Verloc.

Page 73

• Chief Inspector Heat and Winnie.

Page 74

• Stevie. Because she wanted to make sure that Stevie was safe.

Page 81

• That Stevie was the bomber and that Winnie killed Verloc.

After Reading Activities

Comprehension

Pages 90-91

1 a. F (He doesn't seem to have a lot of money)
b. F (Verloc doesn't believe in much, and he's spying on his "friends")
c. T　d. F
e. F (He knows them, but he's not a member of any group)
f. F　g. T　h. DS

i. F (Verloc didn't tell anybody because the action was meant to damage the middle class)

j. T

2 a. the newspapers   b. Ossipon
c. a telegram   d. the newspapers
e. Verloc   f. Winnie
g. Chief Inspector Heat
h. The Assistant Commissioner
i. Winnie

3 a. Winnie and Ossipon
b. Winnie thinks Ossipon knows that Stevie is dead because of Verloc, and that she had to kill Verloc; Ossipon thinks Verloc died in the explosion.
c. Chief Inspector Heat and the Assistant Commissioner.
d. The Assistant Commissioner doesn't want Michaelis to be incriminated because he doesn't want to upset his wife.
e. Chief Inspector Heat is upset; the Assistant Commissioner thinks the Chief Inspector is planning something against him.

③ Characters

Pages 92-93

1 a. F b. F c. T d. T e. F
f. F g. T h. T

2 Possible answers:
a. Verloc, Mr. Vladimir, Ossipon
b. Mr. Vladimir, the Professor
c .Verloc, Mr. Vladimir, Ossipon, the Professor,
d. Winnie, Stevie
e. Stevie
f. Verloc, Ossipon, Winnie
g. Ossipon
h. Winnie

3 1. g 2. f 3. h 4. a 5. d
6. c 7. b 8. e

4 Stevie's father did that to him/used hot iron on Stevie's skin.

④ Vocabulary

Pages 94-95

1
• What the criminal does: confess, commit a crime, feel guilt, be a suspect, go to prison, be out on parole
• What the police do: incriminate, investigate, find evidence, arrest (v.)
• Events: confession, execution, sentence, trial, arrest (n.)

3 a. investigate   b. on parole
c. arrest   d. execution   e. guilt
f. incriminate   g. suspect

4 1. b   2. d   3. a   4. e   5. f   6. c

5 a. an outrage   b. legality
c. repression   d. middle class
e. target   f. blow

⑤ Language

Pages 96-98

1 a. arrest, will take
b. goes, will die, will never forgive
c. will explode, give   d. will be, tries
e. asks, will arrest   f. will kill, find

2 a. He was easily distracted by street cats and dogs.
b. When he arrived, he was taken into a small room.
c. The detonator was switched on.
d. Chief Inspector Heat was shocked by what he saw.
e. After Michaelis was released from prison, a rich old lady decided to help him,
f. A policeman was accidentally killed.
g. The Assistant Commissioner was received immediately (by the Home Secretary).
h. Before Mr Verloc could do anything the knife was already planted in his chest (by Winnie).

3 a. We want them to forget their

own rules and principles of legality.

b. He asked his wife to make his apologies.

c. Winnie/She asked her husband to take Stevie with him.

d. Winnie wanted Mr Ossipon to leave with her.

4 a. There were pieces of him everywhere. We had to use a shovel.

b. He whipped the horse because he had to earn his money.

c. Mr Verloc had to go to Europe.

d. She had to hold on to a lamp-post to stop herself from falling.

5 The law is a red-hot branding instrument. Can't you smell and hear the skin of the people burn? They are feeding their greed on the flesh and the warm blood of the people.

6 a. Karl Yundt.

b. That the law leaves a deep mark on people.

c. That people are branded with hot iron.

d. That in the present condition rich people exploit/ use poor people to their advantage.

e. That rich people eat poor people and drink their blood.

f. No, because he understand only the literal meaning of words.

6 Plot and Theme

Pages 99-101

1 a. 4 b. 5 c. 10 d. 6 e. 8 f. 1 g. 2 h. 3 i. 9 j. 7

2 a. 6 b. 2 c. 10 d. 4 e. 8 f. 1 g. 3 h. 5 i. 9 j. 7

3 a. No. b. No.

c. The author told about the explosion and the start of the investigation

first, and then he went back to the scene when Winnie's mother leaves to go to the almshouse.

4 a. Mr. Vladimir.

b. The Professor.

c. Repression.

d. with terrorist attacks

e. Because it will be the start of the disintegration of middle class morality.

f. No, he just wants repression.

g. No. Possible answer: because he describes them as negative characters.

5 a. Stevie's.

b. Yes. Possible answer: because Stevie is the only character who cares for everybody else.

Terrorism

Page 105

Possible answers: Attacks on ordinary people to make them fear that nobody is safe; the aim of repression.

Exam

Pages 106-107

1. b 2. c 3. a 4. c 5. b 6. b

Test

Pages 108-109

1 a. 1 b. 2 c. 1 d. 1

2 a. 3 b. 2 c. 1 d. 4 e. 4 f. 2

國家圖書館出版品預行編目資料

祕密間諜 / Joseph Conrad 著；Donatella Velluti
改寫；劉嘉珮 譯. 一初版. 一[臺北市]：寂天文化,
2018.2 面；公分. 中英對照;
譯自：The Secret Agent

ISBN 978-986-318-652-6 (平裝附光碟片)
　　　1. 英語

805.18   106025349

原著 _ Joseph Conrad

改寫 _ Donatella Velluti

譯者 _ 劉嘉珮

校對 _ 陳珮瑄

編輯 _ 安卡斯

製程管理 _ 洪巧玲

出版者 _ 寂天文化事業股份有限公司

電話 _ +886-2-2365-9739

傳真 _ +886-2-2365-9835

網址 _ www.icosmos.com.tw

讀者服務 _ onlineservice@icosmos.com.tw

出版日期 _ 2018年2月 初版一刷（250101）

郵撥帳號 _ 1998620-0 寂天文化事業股份有限公司